Prai

CW00409444

"In Janet Clare's impressive c
Distance, Lilly, a restless New ⅼⅰⅼⅼ, ⅼ⅛ ⸻⸻ ,
her mother back to Los Angeles to discover she's in fact
the product of a secret fling her mother once had with a
rugged Australian. Following her mother's footsteps to the
Antipodes, Lilly tracks down her mercurial birth father
and lights upon more than she could have imagined. In
propulsive, exacting strokes, Clare deftly moves us through
a time out of time in a faraway place. A taut, compelling
adventure, exploring little known landscapes, and the depth
and breadth of a woman's yearning." DAVID FRANCIS, AUTHOR
OF STRAY DOG WINTER, WEDDING BUSH ROAD, AGAPANTHUS TANGO

"How could you not love a novel set against the Australian
outback? About fierce love, endless longing, ravenous
desire, and the secrets that derail us and ruin others. A
phenomenally moving experience (it's so much more than a
novel), Clare's debut shows a complex web of relationships
that shifts as much as a desert itself—and is just as
gorgeous." CAROLINE LEAVITT, AUTHOR OF CRUEL BEAUTIFUL
WORLD AND THE NEW YORK BESTSELLERS IS THIS TOMORROW AND
PICTURES OF YOU

"When Lilly, rocked by a family secret, agrees to trek
through the Australian outback with her newly-discovered
father, brother, and niece, the terrain is as remote and
unfamiliar as her travelling companions. There in the
crowded vehicle, the torment of past relationships pursues
her—wanting adventure while wanting safety, feeling
cramped and yet never close enough. A poignant and witty
story of survival, trust, and awakening."
SUSAN HENDERSON, AUTHOR OF THE FLICKER OF OLD DREAMS

About the Author

Originally from New York, Janet Clare lives in Los Angeles with her husband and a small dog named for the town of Lucca, Italy. She studied at UC Berkeley and UCLA. *Time is the Longest Distance* is her first novel.

Visit Janet online
janetclare.com

Time is the Longest Distance

Janet Clare

Vine Leaves Press
Melbourne, Vic, Australia

Print Edition
ISBN: 978-1-925417-82-1

Published by Vine Leaves Press 2018
Melbourne, Victoria, Australia

Cover design by Jessica Bell
Interior design by Amie McCracken

A catalogue record for this book is available from the National Library of Australia

For HPB and DLN

"I didn't go to the moon, I went much further—for time is the longest distance between two places." Tennessee Williams, *The Glass Menagerie*

"Love is so short, forgetting so long." Pablo Neruda, *Tonight I Can Write The Saddest Lines*

Prologue

I am somewhere, nowhere, in the middle of the Australian outback, the last place I belong or ever thought I would be. North from the town of Wiluna, following the famous Canning Stock Route 1900km across the arid heart of Australia, and not one thing easy or sane about it.

For a week four of us, along with an overabundance of supplies, have been packed into a pair of six-cylinder diesel Land Cruisers now stuck deep in sand. The odour of warm bodies mixes with the smell of potatoes, grains, and coffee. I think of dunes, but here they're called ridges and run for miles, saw-toothed, and jagged at the top. Steep, sometimes rising fifty feet, crossing them is like trying to climb an ever-shifting three-storey building. Dust is everything and everywhere. Inescapable. It's in the air of the holy hot sun rising and the ungodly cold night. Dust is what I breathe and eat. It tangles my hair and coats my scalp, itching.

I lean against the dug-in all-terrain vehicle, wheels spinning, mind-boggling. How can I, a forty-five-year-old New Yorker who has aspirin delivered, attempt to push what amounts to a condominium with four wheels up and over a mountain of sand in the most Godforsaken wilderness on earth?

"I told you it wasn't a tea party out here," Cameron says.

He smiles, this father, this stranger, with that wicked grin I've come to know in the two short weeks we've known each other. His face appears carved from heavy wood, deeply creased, otherwise unlined, and softened by hazel eyes that droop slightly at the outer edges.

"I'm fine," I say through the grit in my teeth, not fine at all. My head aches, reeling from dirt and heat and cold and him. Cameron pulls himself taller, shoulders back. He looks at me, a faint twitch in one eye that could be a wink, but maybe not. He's sizing me up.

"Why can't we just go around?" I ask, examining a cluster of new bites on my inner arm. Mosquitoes, or the ever-present bush flies or spiders, hopefully not the deadly redback I've been told about.

"Around can be two days," Cameron says. "We can't afford it in supplies."

I realise again how totally dependent we are on our carefully calculated provisions. The isolation here is staggering, like the magnificent desolation of distant planets.

"We'll have to use the tow," Grant says, wiping the back of his hand over his lips. Lips almost too full, resulting in a slight, not unattractive pout. He's taller than his father, although not by much. And Cameron is leaner, harder, where Grant carries a soft layer.

"I've got it covered," Cameron says, stepping in front of his son.

Grant rubs the stubble of his red-gold beard with the back of his hand and turns his baseball cap around.

"The tyre pressure's too high," Cameron says.

"Same in both," Grant says, climbing into the lead cruiser.

"Can't be," Cameron says.

"Is."

I let out a deep sigh as Jen checks her flawless face in her mirrored compact, wraps a pink daisy appliquéd sweater around her shoulders, and slouches in the backseat of the beached cruiser.

Cameron leans in the window on the sleeves of his worn flannel. "Need you at the wheel, young lady."

She rolls her baby blues at her grandfather and climbs over the seat. I stand nearby, unsmiling, hands on my hips.

"What can I do?" I ask, dust settling in the corners of my eyes, under my nails and between my fingers.

"Stay out of the way," Cameron says.

I take a breath, sand sticking to my nostrils, obliterating any sense of smell, and stare down at the hard ground. A land left behind or never found. And me, I'm a moon walker far from my life.

Cameron grabs hold of the cable from the forward cruiser, legs spread, digging in his heels as Grant starts to jump down. "Let me do that."

"Stay where you are," Cameron says. "I was handling stuff like this before you were born." Arms above his head, he holds firm to the cable. It's heavy and he's old, but he drags it within inches of the hitch as Jen guns the engine for the moment when the cable attaches.

Men and machines are exhilarating to me. In the city, I marvel at tightrope walkers on scaffolding high above a new skyscraper. Now, I watch as Cameron guides the cable closer, both engines roaring, then a loud, metal-cracking snap and the cable rips from his hands, blood suddenly streaming down his arms. I scream as Jen leaps from behind the wheel and runs, blonde hair flying, to her grandfather.

Grant slams the brake and climbs down, yelling at Cameron. "Get out of the way."

"The hell I will," Cameron says. "Get back in, I don't have all day."

They calm down, try it again. Cameron clinging now with bloody hands, guiding the cable until it finds its hold and the engines cut with startling silence. He lets go, knees buckling into the sand, then on his feet before I reach him, waving me away. I stand on the sideline, heart racing, staring fascinated at his ruined hands, rough-boned, unfamiliar, as the wind picks up swirling dust to evening. Cameron grabs a roll of bandage from the cruiser, Jen hugs her sweater closer, and Grant rewinds the cable. They seem to know to stay away from the old man. I'm dumbfounded, aghast. Cameron glances at me.

"Don't look so worried," he says, wrapping his hand with the bandage.

"Not me." The dryness catches my throat and I sound unconvincing.

"Things like this happen," he says.

Not where I'm from. Not in the middle of Manhattan. Sand whips my face and I shift my weight, uneasy.

"You're just a fish out of water," he says.

I nod vaguely at the analogy of a fish in the desert, picture myself out of my element, floundering.

One
New York

I gazed at the spiderweb shimmering off the overhead fan and made a mental note on housekeeping while Thomas panted on top of me. I was starving, hungry for eggs or toast. I had to get up. Cinnamon toast sounded good. I took a deep breath, thinking there was something wrong with me. Couldn't be me, had to be him. Uninspired, that's what it was. Fucking uninspired. I was too critical, impatient, unfair, but it was supposed to be good. Or great. Whatever happened to great?

Squirming, I tried to move my numbed right arm pinned under the weight of our bodies.

"Thomas, I can't feel my arm." Claustrophobia quickened into panic.

"What?" he murmured.

"Lift up," I said in a loud whisper.

He did and I pushed the sheets away with my feet, the scent of laundry detergent filling the air. Ten months and the passion had levelled off just the way everyone always said it would. The exchange rate being a companionable evenness. But I didn't want to level off. I wanted piercing exhilaration, I wanted to tingle and glow. I wanted everything.

The phone rang and I fumbled for the receiver in the faint light. Thomas held his ground.

"Lilly?" My mother's voice, anxious and loud. "Are you sleeping?"

I checked the digital. "It's six o'clock," I said.

Thomas let up but not out.

"I thought you'd be awake," she said, without apology. "I need you to come here, to come home."

Home was where I was. "Is someone dead?" My voice was husky.

"What a thing to say. Do you have a cold?"

I ignored the question, then realised my mother was calling at three in the morning, L.A. time.

"What's wrong?" I asked.

"I can't explain," she said.

"What do you mean? Why can't you tell me?" I could just make out Thomas's intelligent forehead, his slightly receding hairline.

"I can't discuss it on the phone," she said.

In the background, something rustled, like she was getting dressed.

"It's freezing there, isn't it?" she asked, putting the hold button on whatever crisis was at hand. "I heard on the news. I don't know why you live there."

I didn't answer. Thomas licking one ear and my mother yakking in the other was like having a horde of bees around my head.

"That weather's dangerous. You get sick too much," she said.

"I like it here," I said. I'd lived a lifetime in the mildness of Los Angeles. It was where I met Stephen, where we married, and where it ended. But I'd grown sick to death of mild, craving a place with some tangible history, something to hold onto, and returned to New York where I was born.

"Why won't you tell me what's wrong?" I asked. Having what passed for a conversation with my mother while Thomas was on top of me was bizarre enough to almost be erotic.

She paused, too quiet too long for Ida.

"Trust me, it's important," she said. "I need you to come."

I knew the feeling.

"I'll see what I can do," I said and hung up, positive my mother had never before used the word trust.

Another frigid day dawned, ice forming on the window edge. The possibly French armoire with its mirrored façade, five-dollar-wicker rocker, and the discarded clothes from the night before took shape in the snow-white light of morning. Thomas grunted and moved off me, strands of my hair sticking to his face.

"What's going on?" he asked.

The moisture from our bodies grew cool and I pulled up the comforter. I felt my brows knot in that way I knew would leave lines.

"My mother sounds weird," I said, suddenly convinced she was sick and she was never sick, so it had to be serious. So serious she couldn't tell me on the phone.

Thomas got up, walking and scratching to the bathroom. He'd be in and out of the shower and dressed in his predictable blue suit in twenty minutes. I stared at the painting hanging crookedly on the far side of the room and thought about Stephen in his paint-splattered Levi's and tee-shirt, scuffed loafers.

One of his earliest works and one of the few left to me, the abstract blues slashed with mud-brown always made me think of a mean ocean. I remembered everywhere it hung in every home we'd ever lived, how he'd carried it when we moved from one side of the park to the other in Los Angeles. Obscured by its size, hands grasping the outer edges, two legs visible below, he was a walking work of art, carefully avoiding foul balls and toddlers. Twenty years of packing and unpacking, hanging pictures in just the right spot, setting out seashells from long-ago walks. Cartons of books stuffed into shelves. All our worldly goods, what made us, resting together in the same place. Sometimes three years or four, the last nearly thirteen. And then, as though the earth quaked, everything shifted, shaken from its moorings to settle at one end of the world or another, or lost completely.

Thomas straightened his perfectly knotted rep tie. I hadn't moved, waiting for him to finish and leave.

"Dinner later?" he asked, making his exit, signalling with thumbs up.

I agreed and mentally packed a suitcase. If I was going to do this, fly across the country to see my mother, I needed to do it quickly. I'd leave tomorrow, knowing it would cost a fortune on such short notice.

***

The fifth storm of the season had passed through the city, leaving the morning cold and slushy and turning a simple walk around the block into an Olympic event. I stepped gingerly onto the iced pavement, death on my mind.

I wasn't surprised when my father, Herb, died three years ago. He'd always been a nice, soft-spoken man, hardly a presence when alive, so a heart attack in the night had seemed somehow perversely natural. "He went quietly," my mother said, and everyone else repeated it at the funeral, still tiptoeing around so as not to disturb him.

My mother was different. I never thought anything could kill Ida. I didn't think germs could live in her body. And, what would life be like without her? Without her proprietary airs, emotional selfishness, her seemingly innocent remarks served with a side order of disapproval.

"Where's your talent?" she asked me, watching a seven-year-old dancing up a storm on T.V. I was nine, unformed and without any discernible ability.

Things between us had always been strained, pureed, and I was never sure why. Though maybe it was simply because I was her third daughter and she'd just had enough.

Snow piled high at the street corners as I threaded my way through a watery path and turned my head against the wind, my own mortality staring me in the face. I'd seen enough friends die young to know that in the long run, all I wanted was a long run.

I spent most of the day drinking coffee and staring out my office window at falling snow. It had been ten years since I left Los Angeles, and goodbye and good luck to me. I loved New York, and I'd become proficient at holding on, maintaining the magnificent daylight confidence of a capable woman. It was the evenings, the loveliest and saddest time of day, that could shake me. Often alone, I'd go to movies or dinner, anything to keep from going home too soon. Sometimes, I'd stop at the bar of a favourite restaurant, somewhere small and noisy enough. A woman could do that in this town without looking like a hooker, or forever pitifully alone, but not regularly and not always at the same place. At Gino's, the cherub-faced maître'd greeted me warmly and I'd sit on a high-back stool and look over the narrow room, wallpapered with prancing zebras as it had been for forty years. I'd pretend I was just stopping by before meeting someone, somewhere. Then, as evening turned to night, and warmed by alcohol, I'd breathe a sigh of relief. Night would become morning, and I knew I would make it through and go on.

Now, my mother still weighing on my mind, I watched the frosted afternoon slip by. Aside from her weekly bridge game, I had no idea what she did with her evenings. Maybe she cooked a simple dinner, a small piece of fish or chicken purchased whole and divided into single portions. Something I'd never done and never would, the idea of opening the refrigerator to face a foil-wrapped packet more dismal than I could bear. Ida would set a place at the table, arrange her plate, fold a napkin. She'd wrap a sweater around her shoulders and read the paper, chewing her food slowly, as she'd always cautioned me to do. Afterward, she'd make a cup of tea with lemon, watch television, then climb into bed where she slept soundly, hardly disturbing the blankets. My mother had lived a serene life. There had been a time when she travelled the world with Herb in tow. She'd send back postcards and return with souvenirs as though exotic trinkets would somehow make up for indifferent parenting.

Outside my window, traffic slowed, headlights and streetlights blinked on. I pulled down the sleeves of my favourite cardigan and leaned on my elbows. My eyes felt sunken, my skin dehydrated from too much caffeine. Down the hall, secretaries changed into boots and wrapped scarves around their necks, office doors slammed shut, keys turned and footsteps clicked toward the elevator. The day was done. Get out, catch the train, the bus, hunt for the phantom taxi before the snow hit hard.

Distracted, my eyes scanned across to an office window where a slim man approached a young woman and shut the door behind him. He locked the door as the woman got up, tugging at her tight skirt, and they met in a fast embrace. I took a breath, riveted by this city tableau. The man pulled the woman closer, his arms encircling her, and I was right there with them, swept up in their drama until the lights dimmed, and I finally turned away.

The air in my office had grown stale along with the coffee, fluorescent lights hummed overhead, the halls abruptly quiet. I got up with an effort after hours of inactivity and grabbed my coat.

On the street, icy wind spiked my face as my boots crushed new snow.

Thomas was in our customary booth, drinks on the table. I took off my coat and slid along the cool leather beside him.

"Aren't you cold?" he said by way of greeting. "Such a thin coat." He held the fabric between two fingers.

"I'm fine." I smiled, fluffed my hair. An image of the woman in the window flashed through my mind, wondering if she was all right, feeling responsible, imagining a newspaper headline of ultimate disaster. I looked at Thomas over my vodka. A cuddly bear, he smelled good and he was big and real sitting here with his whiskey in front of him.

When I first met Thomas, his protective, take-charge manner was a relief, but somewhere along the way it became overbearing. Still, he was kind. Happily divorced from a brittle, bottle blonde, he said he didn't miss her for a minute, which I found difficult to believe, but envied him. His daughter, Ivy, lived in Wyoming with a guy named Guy and raised heifers. Thomas visited at round-up a while ago and came back distressed that his beautiful, educated daughter seemed content to clean up after cloven-hoofed animals.

"Whatever floats her boat," I said.

Thomas didn't agree. I thought this indicative of some basic socio-political ideals we didn't have in common. He often referred to me as a leftover, left-wing-Berkeley-pinko-Communist, although I'd never joined anything since the Girl Scouts. He was a Republican, though not fanatic, not one of those, and a money manager. What else. I wanted adventure, to go down the Amazon, to visit Patagonia and Antarctica. He didn't. Then again, he said he loved me and he cared that my coat wasn't warm enough.

"I think my mother's sick, maybe dying," I said.

He told me not to jump to conclusions. But that's what I always did. Jumping, leaping. We studied our drinks. The restaurant, recently remodelled, was hard-edged and slick with lights like parachutes suspended from the ceiling. I felt out of place even though it was our place. Thomas relaxed easily into the black leather.

"Whatever happens, it's time you made some investments, think about your future," he said. It was an old song. My job at a non-profit paid enough to live poorly in a rich city. He pulled at his shirt cuffs so there was an even amount of white showing from his jacket.

"I've never been fond of the future," I said. I'd wanted to be a painter, even went to art school. But Stephen had been the real talent and there never seemed to be enough room under the same roof, or maybe not enough paint.

We ordered another drink, salads, and grilled salmon. Everyone in New York ate salad and grilled salmon while the rest of the country chewed happily on whole cows and pounds of potatoes. The restaurant grew louder, and I looked over the sea of suits and thought of all the years I'd attached my success to the man I loved. History was littered with women who had given up their desires for the so-called greater good, the better artist. Sometimes though, you lost it all. Your own dreams and those you shared.

Thomas squeezed lemon on his salad. I piled on bleu cheese.

"Maybe I'll go back to painting," I said.

"Great," he said without interest, pointing to my salad with his fork. "That fat's going to go straight to your heart."

Yeah, well. Something should, I thought.

Two

I arrived in L.A. on one of those grey days when it's hard to tell if it's morning or evening. Low fog, or smog leftover from the '70's, melted into the hazy sunshine of mid-afternoon. I picked up the emerald-green rental car and headed north on the 405. To the east, on a hill above automobile dealerships, was a cemetery with an eternally flowing waterfall. To the west, the newest, biggest dung-coloured shopping-movie-multiplex. A gauze veneer hung over the city, adding to the allure and distraction. There was nothing completely clear about Los Angeles. A place without definition, it could be whatever you wanted it to be, or nothing at all.

I normally didn't respond so readily to my mother's beck and call, but she'd never really asked before. Not like this. Her requests were usually much more oblique, as though she was never really sure what she wanted from me. "When will I see you?" she'd ask before listing her busy schedule, how she might fit me in. And, as much as she complained about my living three thousand miles away, sometimes I thought she preferred it.

I rolled down the windows and let the warm air tangle my hair, remembering when I was fifteen and driving up the coast with my mother to visit her crazy aunt who lived in a Pacifica sanatorium. My mother talked non-stop the entire trip with only an occasional thirty-second lull, which I timed.

"Evelyn was never a favourite of mine," she'd said. "Even before she went nuts."

"Then why are we going?" I'd asked, looking out the window and wishing she'd slow down so I could jump out.

"We all have to do things we may not want to do."

"That's just hypocritical," I'd said. Hypocrite was my pet new word. "I would never do anything unless I really wanted to."

She said I'd find out differently and I stared out the window, envying the grazing cows.

***

Now, as if cued for my arrival, the Beach Boys sang "Good Vibrations" and I sang along, woefully out of tune. It was two o'clock, a stupid time to arrive anywhere, too early for cocktails and dinner, and sleep. Instead, I'd be pitched into immediate conversation with Ida, which meant a rundown on the weather and recent deaths of people I didn't know.

"I'm glad you're not late," my mother said, opening the door to the blinding light of her Santa Monica condo. She gave me a quick hug. Had I grown or was she always so petite?

"Late for what?" I asked, dragging my bag behind me.

She didn't answer, turned, and kept on going down the narrow entryway, the heels of her patent-leather shoes clacking on the marble floors. I followed her into the living room, a burst of lime green and yellow, the glare bouncing off white laminated tables. Ida favoured bright colours in contrast to her dour personality, decorating as if to please someone she'd rather be.

There was a welcoming aroma of chicken with garlic, probably roasted potatoes, and I knew there'd be something green, broccoli or asparagus, a tossed salad. My mother was a good cook. I dropped my bags, feeling like a black cloud descending on the sunshine, and looked around for the few remnants from my childhood. The glass horse figurines with flowing black manes and eyes that followed you, the alabaster clock with hands made from keys. When I was a kid I always wanted to break open that clock, take out the keys, and try to find a door to open.

"You made good time," she said, walking toward the kitchen, separated from the living room by a counter of stone mosaics. "Sometimes there's traffic, but you made good time."

My mother had a habit of repeating herself, no doubt thinking that as long as words floated around the room, everyone was happy. Always a fast mover, she'd hardly slowed down with age. Slender, dressed in apricot pants with a matching silk shirt, her hair beige and short, she wore gold earrings, little makeup. There was a new roundness to her shoulders I hadn't noticed before, remembering how she used to poke me in the back to stand up straight.

"Always in black," she said and looked at me over her shoulder as she grabbed the coat I'd dropped on the sofa. "I'll just hang this up."

She was already halfway down the hall before I could stop her, and I tried not to act exasperated as I caught a quick glimpse of myself in the mirror above the creamy sectional. When I left New York in the morning, I thought I looked pretty good, even stylish, but now, seeing myself through my mother's eyes, I was suddenly the lead in an Italian funeral. I sat on the sofa and pulled a lipstick from my bag. She walked back into the room.

"Could you tell me what this is all about?"

She ignored my question and tied an apron embroidered with bees and the word busy around her waist. "What do you want to drink?"

"Vodka, but I'll settle for a Diet Coke." My mother never even kept a bottle of wine in the house.

"Alcohol makes you old," she said, reaching for a glass.

"You get old anyway," I said.

"Not always." She rinsed an already clean glass and poured the soda.

"What's that supposed to mean?" I asked.

No answer again. The scent of recently sprayed air freshener overpowered the cooking smells and made my eyes water. She was acting strange, and my mother wasn't strange. She was predictable. She'd lived a life of relative ease, apparent contentment. I had no idea if happiness had ever entered into it.

I got up and filled my glass with ice. "What's going on?" I asked again, then softened my voice. "Are you sick?"

"Not yet," she said. She stood on the kitchen side of the counter and rearranged the napkin holder, the pepper mill, refolded a towel.

I was used to her constant moving, although now she seemed more erratic than usual. I took a long drink, shook the ice in my glass, and sat back again, trying to imagine what could be wrong. A nice, dark family secret might be fun, I thought, watching her fuss around the kitchen. My hand felt a loose thread on the sofa and I noticed how the sorbet-hued condo, normally kept to gleaming perfection, had lost some of its gloss. Every surface was crammed with tokens from various trips my parents had taken together. Shipboard photos of Ida and Herb posed on either side of a life raft from the M/S Harmony or the Starlight Viking Princess. I looked closely at a picture of them bundled in warm coats with a gloomy sky in the background. The man was like a ghost. He could be anyone.

"I have no idea where that was taken," Ida said, without curiosity. "Maybe, Eastern Europe." Far from home, they didn't cling to each other or even hold hands. "I have to talk to you before Bitsy and Charlotte get here."

I put the picture down and tried not to groan at the thought of my sisters. Both older, they had married unimaginative men who were good providers, professionals with established lives. They had homes and cars and God-knows-what. I had God-knows-what.

Ida's fingers, lean, the knuckles enlarged, nervously twisted her too big ring, nails painted a soft coral. She ran her hands over the bees, smoothing her apron. She used to send me cute aprons all the time, butterflies and pansies or caricatures of befuddled cooks. I kept them stuffed in drawers, unused.

She poured herself a cup of coffee and we sat at the

dining room table set for dinner. Gold fabric placemats, tumblers turned upside down in the right-hand corner. In the centre of the table was a tangled glass sculpture purchased in Prague.

"We bought it for nothing," she said, wiping off a speck of dust. "Herb hated it."

I wondered if she missed him. Always preoccupied, my father had been the mild-mannered man of a house with four women. He had been a vexillologist. Studying flags and emblems, he'd kept dozens of examples rolled up in his office, along with tons of books on the subject. He would spend hours at it, pasting away, the smell of drying glue crusty on his fingers. It seemed to be the only thing that really interested him.

Ida turned the sculpture around. "I kept it in a closet until after he died," she said, sitting back satisfied somehow to have this ugly thing out in the open. She had a queer little smile on her face. "I've decided a few things lately and one of them is to tell the truth."

A fly buzzed against the glass doors. What truth was she talking about?

She cleared her throat. "Do you remember the story of when I went to Australia?" she asked, not looking at me and not waiting for an answer. "Your sisters were still babies." She bit her lip and went on, her voice was different, softer than I'd ever heard. "They were a handful and I was worn out. Your grandfather suggested I visit his brother in Australia for a rest."

I remembered now and recalled thinking it a remarkable story only because I would have thought of a getaway as a weekend in the Catskills. That she'd left her kids and travelled so far had to be unusual at the time.

She moved her coffee cup away, brought it back. "I was twenty-four," she said. "Australia was the most exciting place I'd ever been." She straightened the placemat and clasped her hands in front of her.

"I met a man," she said, looking down as a pink glow appeared on her cheeks. Something I'd never noticed before, this rose tint spreading over her fragile skin, embarrassed like a young girl. "He was nice looking and he took a shine to me." She paused, looked up, but not at me, blinking. "I was pretty then." She lifted a hand to her brow as if to adjust the picture in her mind. "I was."

I took a sip of Coke, swallowing hard. I'd been shopping for shrouds, already felt guilty for not missing her. The idle thought I'd had of something potentially dark and hidden now crept over me.

"What are you talking about?" I asked, though maybe I knew too well what she was getting at. I pictured someone like Katherine Hepburn in trousers and tousled hair, my mind confused with images of my mother, either sick and dying or floating down a river with Humphrey Bogart.

She stared at the table then raised her head, her eyes lacklustre, the colour quickly draining from her skin. She sighed as though she'd given up or given in and, now, seeking relief, her words came in a rush. "I had an affair with him," she said.

I stared stupidly at her as if she'd spoken a foreign language. My mother, an *affair*? Stone-cold Ida? I had affairs, not my mother, a woman who had never talked about sex.

She hesitated, focusing on the cup in front of her.

"I got pregnant." Her voice barely a whisper, she took a breath. "Cameron Washinsky, his name." She swallowed hard. "He's your real father."

It took an effort to keep my mouth from hanging open as my ears flooded with the words. *Real. Father.* I felt a sudden ache deep in my stomach that went through to my back.

"I wanted to tell you," she said, still not looking at me. "Many times." She stopped, stretched her fingers, then interlaced them as though she might pray. Outside, the sun broke through and blasted white on the stone balcony, a single plant dead in a corner.

I didn't move. I just stared down at the stupid lime green carpet. What was she saying, was she kidding? All those years of useless talk about weather, clothes, what to have for lunch. And there was *this*? Out of the corner of my eye, her face appeared calm, even serene.

"I was afraid you'd hate me," she said. Her eyes, dark and naturally deep set, seemed to sink further.

I looked past her to the too-bright patio. "That plant needs water," I said as if to deny the present. I thought of Stephen, shirtless on a hot day, running the garden hose up and over our balcony; what street was that?

Ida turned to look outside and I got up and wandered over to the family photographs, touching them lightly like an archaeologist discovering alien bones. Dust swirled in the sunlight. My mother had always been a meticulous housekeeper, and the dust always came back. There were photos of my sisters, little girls with curly hair, and me off to one side, so different, looking out from somewhere else. I'd never noticed that distance before, and now, moving from one picture to another, I realised the man I'd called my father wasn't in any of them. Nowhere to be seen. Had he always been the photographer? Then I remembered a rare, early photograph taken of Herb with me as a child that showed an uncomfortable man standing stiffly, as though posing with a cardboard cut-out of fun.

"I know I shouldn't have waited so long," Ida said, her voice startling me. "But it doesn't matter. I'm too old and tired to pretend anymore."

The air had thinned, my throat tightened. What did she mean it didn't matter? What *did* matter? She continued, and I listened through the dense fog that filled my head. When she'd returned to California and found she was pregnant, she wrote to Cameron and said her husband had agreed to raise me with their other daughters.

Just like that? How was that possible? Had he agreed so readily? *Why?* I blinked as though it would clear my brain. How could she have been so positive I wasn't Herb's child? She hadn't been gone that long, had they stopped sleeping together? It was something I really didn't want to think about.

"Herb was a good man," she said. "He took care of me, of us, but Cameron was different."

Of course, he was. Other men were always different. "Was he married, too?" I asked. Why was that my first real question?

"Yes, with a son," she said.

I was dazed, like I'd been slapped in the face or hit by a truck, glad not to have had the vodka, although I'd need it soon. Why wasn't she throwing herself hysterically at my feet, begging forgiveness? And, why wasn't I screaming at her, what the *fuck*? Who was this Cameron? Washinsky? Sounded Russian, or Polish. Where was he from? Or his father before him. Where was *I* from?

"Do you know where he is?" I asked, too calm. Was he even alive?

"I'm not sure," she said. "I assume still in Australia." A few slow tears ran down her cheeks. "You know, it's strange, the secret filled me up for such a long time." She sighed, pulled a tissue from her apron pocket and wiped her eyes. "And now, I just feel empty."

So, this woman, who I couldn't remember ever telling me anything about how she felt other than disappointed, now, on a perfectly normal, horrible LA day, with the threat of Santa Ana winds hot, dry, and homicidal, tells me the man I grew up with wasn't my father at all, but just a nice guy making the best of things, and *she* feels empty?

"Why are you finally telling me this now?" I asked.

She looked at her hands, visibly aged, the skin translucent with a network of veins. "Well, you know, no one lives forever," she said.

Great. She wasn't dying, but she might? Sometime. And so, like a relay, she was handing off the anguish. Here, you carry this for a while. Yet with it all, I still couldn't imagine how she'd pulled it off. Living with Herb, sleeping with him, and all the while carrying another man's baby, and he *knew*? I had to admire her even in my own fury at being deceived.

The doorbell rang and she stood, pulling at her sleeves. "That must be your sisters."

"You're kidding. Here? Now?" I stayed where I was, rooted by astonishment.

"I had to tell them, too," she said pleadingly, backing away.

"You told them before you told *me*?" I'd started to feel some sympathy for her. I must have been crazy.

The sun moved and the condo turned orange.

"I was afraid," she said. Seemingly more composed, nearly her old self again, she opened the door to Charlotte and Bitsy's shrill entrance.

Was she afraid I'd scream and carry on? She needed reinforcements?

My sisters lowered their voices, no easy feat, as if entering a sickroom, mumbling in the hallway until Bitsy, dressed in head-to-toe banana yellow, jollied in and flapped over to me on tiny backless shoes.

Ida sat down and faded into the sofa.

"Don't you just look great? Love those boots," Bitsy said. She was the cheerleader sister, professionally buoyant, as though riding a float in a perpetual parade. Only eighteen months apart, I'd never understood how we could be so different. At least that was cleared up.

I didn't say anything. I didn't have to because hard on her heels was Charlotte, still talking and looking shorter than the last time I'd seen her. She ran her tongue over her teeth smeared with red lipstick and looked me up and down. "You've lost weight," she said.

Coming from her, it didn't sound like a compliment. I felt myself falling back into that miserable teenage tension and tried to remember I was a grownup who didn't live here anymore. Charlotte collapsed her over-stuffed body into an over-stuffed chair close to me.

"We know everything," she said, pulling at her dark curls.

"What a relief," I said.

"It's hard to believe, but we understand." Her nearness, heavy perfume, and jangle of bracelets were oppressive. "We think Dad was wonderful, accepting you."

Charlotte never failed to amaze.

"Fuck you," I said, keeping my voice low and even. I wanted to punch her in the face like I'd always wanted ever since we were kids.

I gestured toward Ida, who appeared calm and bewildered. "Have you even thought about what this woman went through?" I asked. Not having thought about it myself for more than twenty minutes, it felt odd, but necessary, to defend her.

"I was just trying to be nice," Charlotte said. Red lips pursed, she pulled at her tight skirt, took out a file, and smoothed a nail. "Have it your way."

"My way is fuck you."

"Lilly, please," Ida said.

"Right, Mom, watch your language, but not who you screw," I said. I felt like throwing a rock through the sliding glass doors.

Bitsy, silent and wide-eyed, moved to the sofa where Ida had nearly disappeared and put her arm around our mother. Good, I thought, you comfort her.

"I think we should all just take a breath and figure

this out," Charlotte said.

"Exactly what do you think needs figuring?" I asked. "That my mother lied to me my entire life?" My voice got higher, my throat strained.

"You should calm down," Charlotte said, checking her nails.

"That's out of the question." I got up. "I have to get out of here." I felt the tautness in my neck and glanced at my mother, who looked like she'd been struck.

"Don't leave," Ida said, her voice small, beaten. "We have to talk."

"Maybe some other time," I said. "Without the crowd."

Well aware of the Cinderella aspect of my two older sisters, I'd spent far too much of my childhood vying for their love and attention which never materialized. Now, I walked down the hall, grabbed my bags and, hot as it was, pulled on my coat. Leaving my mother with Charlotte and Bitsy was like throwing her to the wolves and I knew I was being dramatic, but this called for drama.

Charlotte had moved to the other side of Ida, my loving sisters forming a fortress around her, and the three of them silently watched as I picked up my bags and walked out the door.

I stood on the front step, dizzy in the incessant late afternoon sun. I was scared of what I didn't know, and excited, too. I stumbled to the car and got in, the heat and quiet enveloping me. I always knew there was something, didn't I? I would have been less surprised to find out I was adopted, maybe even welcomed it. But what was I supposed to do now? Just go home? Go back to work? I started the engine, laughed out loud. Did I still have to send "to a great sister" birthday cards? And what about the syrupy Mother's Day card Ida always expected? Maybe there's a Father's Day greeting, insipid with golf bags and fishing tackle, for dropout dads.

Three

I hadn't changed clothes in twenty-four hours, my hair was dirty, my face like cardboard. I threw myself on the sofa, relieved to be home. The phone rang and I let it go until the machine picked it up. *It's Mom. Call me. I want to know you're okay.*

It's very simple, just never call her back. It rang again and I waited until I heard Thomas start to leave a message and answered it. "Meet me for a drink," I said.

The night air forced me awake as I walked the few blocks past familiar falafel huts, Bob's Pizza, and chic boutiques. Everything was the same, except for me. The tiny Italian restaurant hummed, quietly pleasant in the lull between dinner and after-theatre; Thomas waiting, drinks on the table. I was happy to see him.

Late as it was, he still had on his navy-blue suit, although he'd loosened his tie. His idea of casual. There were two small spots on his chin where he'd nicked himself shaving. I liked him better with a few imperfections. Sometimes, it seemed his posture was too straight, his clothes too neat. We kissed briefly.

"What's up?" he asked. He pulled off his tie, rolled it precisely around his hand and stuffed it in a pocket, then sipped his drink and listened patiently while I told him the story. The telling didn't make it seem any less crazy.

"I thought I'd had Ida figured out," I said, slumping back, exhausted and suddenly realizing it wasn't just my father who was unknown to me, but my mother as well. And how much of my own idea of myself was tied into what I'd always thought of her?

There was a shivery sound of glasses being stacked. I took a gulp of my second vodka and ordered another. The waitress, spiky hair and attitude, turned on a kitten heel. She didn't want to get me another drink, she wanted to be a star. Thomas handed me the olives from his martini.

"What kind of man doesn't want to know about his kid?" I asked. "That I never heard from him?"

"I think you're going to have to find out for yourself," he said.

"I know," I said, like I did, which I didn't. I was confused and tired.

"You need to think about what you want." Thomas, his organized mind forever putting ducks in a row.

"I don't want anything," I said. "Who needs him, this stranger?"

"That's what you say."

We sat twirling our drinks, condensation pooling the table. The late crowd arrived. Thomas got up and held my coat for me. "Just don't get your hopes up about this guy," he said.

"Why not?" Hope was the best thing about this. Maybe he's a prince, better yet, a genius. I dragged myself out of the booth and stood while Thomas buttoned my coat for me like I was a child or an invalid. I knew there was a risk in knowing the truth, but didn't I owe it to myself to try and meet the person my mother had kept secret? Who had kept himself secret from me?

Days went by. Snow melted as cracks of sunlight filtered through the dirty iced city. Bitsy sent a note, breezy and detached, never mentioning recent events. Nothing from Charlotte, which didn't surprise me. As the youngest child, I'd been mystified and lonely, solemnly tagging after my sisters who either tolerated or resented me. I'd spent years pretending it didn't matter, that I was stronger and better. But now the loneliness returned like an illness I thought I had conquered, familiar and frightening.

Ida called every few days, apologizing as I hurried to get off the phone. We'd never had a real conversation, why start now? Greeting cards had been her preferred means of communication, a habit she vainly tried to bestow on me. "Send a nice card," she'd say.

Try to find the Hallmark for this one, I thought, furious with her for every bad childhood moment. But this was beyond all that. I was faced with a woman capable of the long lie and my anger alternated with guilt as I recalled her face when I'd left her in L.A. It wasn't just a matter of forgiving her or not. She wasn't the same person anymore. And, of course, neither was I.

***

I thought back to four years ago when I'd taken a couple days off and wound up in Los Angeles. God knows why. Some foolish attempt at family unity. Charlotte was already married to Stan, the fat paediatrician, while Bitsy, dragging around multiple small dogs, continued her quest for her third, perfect husband.

It was noon, and we were on our way to pick up our mother for what Ida liked to call a girl's day. The weather, as usual, was brilliant sunshine. Our faces shined with perspiration, makeup blending, lipstick bleeding.

Outside Ida's condo, Charlotte leaned on the car horn and my mother, sporting a vibrant Pucci print, stepped to her balcony and waved. A few minutes later, she rattled her house keys at the open car window.

"Here I am, girls." She got in on the passenger side. "You can stop talking about me now."

Bitsy and I sat in the back seat. I closed my eyes.

"This is a German car, isn't it?" Ida asked, slamming the front passenger door. "I'm looking for the button for the window."

"It's a BMW," Charlotte answered. "You know that."

"I like a Buick or a Lincoln," she said. She found the button and closed the window, narrowly missing her colour-coordinated scarf.

"Hope you're ready to shop," Bitsy said.

"I don't need anything," Ida answered, patting the side of her hair.

The car reeked from a mix of perfumes. My head started to ache.

"We'll have lunch first," Charlotte said, making an illegal U-turn and heading toward the beach. Dangling gold earrings flew about her neck.

"I'm not hungry," Ida said. "Your appetite changes when you get older, you know."

"This was your idea," I said. "Lunch and shopping."

"I know," Ida said. "I could use a hat. Why don't people wear hats anymore? They wear hats in New York, don't they Lilly?"

"In the winter," I said.

"And some makeup," she said, taking out a hand mirror. "A bright lipstick."

"Fine," I said. "A hat and lipstick."

Charlotte had a heavy foot and in minutes, she pulled up to the curb on Ocean Avenue, stopped at a meter, and grabbed the handicap placard from its hiding place. Charlotte had a bad hip. We got out. Bitsy, a vision in violet with a tiny designer bag on her arm, held the restaurant door open and we followed a girl in tight pants and hair twisted in a dark mess to a table on the far side of the room.

"They've stuck us in the corner," my mother said, sitting.

"Would you like to move?" I asked.

"No."

We ordered salads. Ida ordered coffee.

"You eat," she said. "I'm just here for the company." She held up her hand and squinted. "That light has such a glare." She twisted in her seat, looking around. "Do you know what happened to my sweater? I feel a chill."

I picked her sweater off the floor and handed it to her. She held her fork aloft then helped herself to my chicken salad. "Your sisters and I are worried about you, Lilly," she said. "Since the divorce from what's-his-name." She took a bite and chewed, looking around the table. "Well, I don't have to remember it anymore."

"*We're* not worried," Charlotte interrupted. "Mom is." She buttered another piece of French bread, smacking her lips as she ate and glanced at me. "I'm sure you're happy as a lark living the single life in New York City."

"Being single is awful," Bitsy said, reaching across to touch my hand in sisterly sympathy. I pulled away.

"You need to find someone, Lilly, that's all," Ida said. "Otherwise, you'll end like cousin Rita in Miami, spending all your time playing canasta."

I held my tongue at my mother's cliché of a woman alone and left town the following day.

***

After a brief internet search, I located an address for Cameron in Melbourne, which I thought was a good omen, and wrote to him right away. Maybe I could have called or emailed, but I wanted something back, a piece of paper, a signature, or maybe I just wanted it to take more time. It had been three weeks.

Thomas sprawled across my denim sofa, one loafer dangling from his foot.

"He's still alive," I said, walking in with the mail. I held out the letter. "From his son. His father would like to meet me, I should come down, he says. Like it's a flight of stairs."

Thomas was concentrating on how far out on the edge of his toe he could balance his shoe. "Don't be so hostile," he said. "Maybe he'll surprise you."

I gave him a hard look. "You know you don't just fill up that sofa," I said, apropos of nothing. "You fill up this whole apartment."

His shoe fell to the floor. Unflappable, he sat up. "Are you going to pack that chip on your shoulder?"

"Very funny."

"You know you're going."

He was right.

"I feel like I got on a wrong bus somewhere," I said. "Reminds me of that story about the father who put his infant in a carrier on top of the car and then drove off. I feel like someone forgot I was on the roof."

I sat on one of the rattan bar stools. There wasn't a bar and it was really only one room with a slice of kitchen, tiny bathroom; white walls, blue-striped pillows, baskets, and old quilts, kind of Malibu-east.

Thomas came over and put his arms around me. "You buy a ticket, get on the plane, meet this so-called father, and come home," he said.

"Life is so simple for you, isn't it?"

"Your life."

I made a face at him and straightened the crushed sofa pillows. "We're all good at everyone else's life," I said. "Maybe I don't want to go. Screw this creep who never gave a shit."

"That's always an option," he said.

I stopped, pillow in hand. "Now, you think I shouldn't go?"

"That's not what I said. It's your decision." He put on his jacket and opened the door, letting in the spicy aroma of assorted ethnic cooking from the five other apartments on the floor. "Get your passport in order," he said, kissing my cheek, he left.

***

I pulled out an old suitcase and came across a post-card Stephen and I had sent to ourselves. It was Sunday afternoon, New York gloom outside, ideal conditions to sift through the sad, sweet stockpile of our past. I did this to myself every once in a while, just to see if I could take it. I had a large box of photographs too, but I needed a snowstorm for those.

We had sent the card from Mont St Michel in France, with the message, *"Wish we were here!"* We were young, and it would be trite but true to say the world had been ours. We forgot about the card until it arrived months later reminding us, as it reminded me now, of the town of Avranches. How we'd toured the monastery and ate the famous omelette whipped in a copper bowl. Copper was supposed to make the eggs taste sweeter, and it was true.

That night, we went to dinner and drank more wine than usual, which was a lot in those days, then walked back through empty streets to our room overlooking a garden of roses where we made drunken love, falling over each other. In the morning, heads in an alcohol haze, we dragged our bags to the car, which had disappeared. We stared at the spot where it should have been like it would return if we just looked harder. Had our cheap little rental car been stolen? There seemed no other explanation.

But this was France, so there was no need to hurry, and we stayed in the garden, winter sun on our faces, and had our morning coffee. Then another, and maybe one more, and with time and clarity came a revelation. We retraced our steps from the night before and across from the restaurant, we found the car nobody else wanted. Neither of us remembered having taken it to dinner.

"Well, we had two bottles," I said.

"Three," Stephen corrected me.

Now, as thunder rolled through the city, I sat on the floor and stared at the yellowed postcard. I wondered if we had come across this happy souvenir during the drama of our breakup, would we have stopped long enough to remember who we had been. Would it have helped us to go on?

***

It was dinnertime in LA when I called my mother. I thought I owed it to both of us to try to have a conversation.

"I was just fixing myself a salad," Ida said. I could tell she was balancing the receiver on her shoulder and eating something.

"I'm thinking of going to Australia," I said, looking outside my kitchen window at the multitude of other windows bright as Christmas in the clear night.

She didn't say anything. There was a sound of a bowl hitting the granite counter, a fork on glass, something being stirred. I leaned against the sink and waited until she stopped chewing.

"You heard from him?" she asked.

"His son answered my letter. His father would like to meet me."

"The son," she said the word slowly. "Of course. A grown man, now."

"You never heard anything from Cameron? No letters?"

"No," she said. "Nothing."

What did it mean to her, to have never had a word from him? I wondered if she'd tried to contact him again. Wouldn't I? Maybe she did, and he never responded. Something she wouldn't want to admit.

"When will you go?" she asked.

"I'm not sure," I said. "Soon, though."

"I guess you have to."

"Isn't there anything more you could tell me?" I asked.

"It was a long time ago, Lilly," she said. "And right now, I have a terrible headache."

It had taken her my whole life to tell me the truth, or maybe part of the truth, so why should I expect further information to be any easier? We hung up and I checked online for flights to Melbourne.

Four

I'd loaded myself down with every distraction I could think of for the long flight. Books. Music. It didn't help. I couldn't read or listen to anything. Sleep was impossible. I just sat, trying to imagine what I couldn't. The man I would meet. Then, if I closed my eyes, or even if I didn't, I would suddenly remember Stephen's hands. Slender, scrubbed, rolling the ring on his middle finger, hands on his hips or deep in his pockets, on my shoulder; gestures I didn't know I'd memorized.

I landed, nervous and exhausted, and almost passed by the young woman holding up a yellow sheet of paper with my name on it. She offered her hand along with a gorgeous smile.

"I'm Jennifer, Grant's daughter," she said and told me to call her Jen.

Bright-eyed, tall, and angular. I looked at her dumbly.

"Cameron's granddaughter," she explained. "My dad sent me, hope you don't mind."

"Not at all," I said, trying to be nonchalant. Nervous enough about meeting my half-brother, who knew he had a daughter? I followed her through the grey-green light of the airport. She was a beauty, my new niece, maybe twenty-three years old, in faded jeans and tee-shirt, and the graceful walk of an athlete. A swimmer, I thought, or tennis, volleyball, maybe even soccer.

"My father's nervous," she said, ponytail swaying.

"Glad to hear it," I said. I'd declined Grant's invitation to stay at his house, thinking it wise not to push the closeness. He hadn't mentioned a wife, never said *we*. I stared, mesmerized as the baggage carousel circled, smooth and quiet.

Outside, it was bright as LA

"This is so cool," Jen said, tossing my bag in the back of an aged station wagon. "I don't have any other aunts."

I smiled at her, relieved to know there weren't more relatives. I had enough problems with those I'd left in California. I didn't need trouble on a whole other continent.

She shifted gears and we jerked forward. "Sorry, I'm better with trucks."

It wasn't long before we turned into a narrow drive bordered by dusty eucalyptus. "I grew up in this house," she said. "But I have my own flat in the city." Instead of slowing, she stepped on the gas. The trees flew by.

The overarching branches created a shaded gateway that led to a faded white house with a wide wrap-around porch, yellow roses winding along the railing and up the balusters. A tall, loose-limbed man pushed through the screen door, three dogs, rangy as their master, at his heels. Jen careened, brakes screeching, and stopped the car inches from the fence. The man took big steps, his arms propelling him awkwardly, his clothing carelessly dishevelled, giving him the appearance of an overgrown kid bewildered at his size.

Wildflowers threatened the pathway and he kicked at the gravel, then held up his hand to shield his eyes from the sun as he approached the car. There was something familiar in his purposeful walk, and I followed his gaze beyond the garden to the trees and further to the fields.

Jen jumped out, rushing to her father and the dogs, and I sat, anxious, yet unable to move until Grant was beside me, leaning with both hands on the door. Rolled sleeves revealed light hair on his forearms; on his right wrist, a watch with a worn leather band. He's left-handed, I thought, like me. He had a goofy smile in an imperfect face and there was a thickness to his features as though put on with a palette knife. He had high cheekbones, a full mouth, and I thought how pretty those lips would be on a woman.

"I've been waiting for you," he said. Taking a step back, he opened the car door to let me out.

"I'm on time," I said, checking my watch without focussing.

The dogs turned circles in the yard.

"Late by a lifetime," he said.

A scruff of beard, brown eyes that didn't waver. Grant didn't seem one bit nervous. I smiled weakly at the lovely nasal twang of his accent. "You could say that."

He put his hand on my arm. "Nothing to be afraid of," he said. "Leave that for tomorrow."

"I'm not afraid," I said, aware of his touch and a scent of peppermint and something underneath that reminded me of newsprint and ink.

Giant bees buzzed at my ears as I followed him up the

path, noticing the light stain on his left hand.

"Don't mind them," he said, without stopping. "They won't bother you."

The size of small birds, they bothered me.

Jen was ahead of us, leading the way to the back, and we entered the house through the kitchen. It was a cosy room, although any woman could tell it belonged to a man who lived alone. There was a brown look to it as though something had overcooked a while ago and, along with the coffee rings on the table, had become a part of the décor. It was warm with the scent of burnt toast and honey; the walls covered in plaid paper and wood counters that bore the scars of heavy knives.

The dogs spread out on the brick floor, waiting for whatever dogs waited for. We sat at the round oak table. There was a bottle of vodka and a bucket of ice, and I breathed easier as Grant poured and Jen brought out a plate of cheese and crackers, then sat and stretched her legs on a chair. She looked from me to her father.

"Don't see it," she said, squinting at us. "You two don't look at all alike."

My hair was darker, my skin paler. Grant had the red-brown colouring of the earth. He ran his hands through his hair, his wide forehead appropriately creased. I took a long, slow drink of icy vodka. He poured me another.

"To get you to talk," he said.

I didn't think so. I felt mute. Curious about his wife but afraid to ask. Maybe she was dead. Maybe he killed her, buried her under the steamy floorboards. It seemed like that kind of place. I looked down at my feet, my mind fuzzy from travel. The screen door suddenly slammed shut and Grant got up and secured the latch.

"Wind's picking up," he said.

"Is that normal this time of day?" I asked. As if I'd come here to discuss the weather. I sounded like my mother.

"Nothing's normal down here," he said, smiling like it was a joke and the truth.

Jen picked up her glass. "He's kidding. But you know we do have a lot of weird animals," she said. "Some that belong to the country club."

"The most poisonous snakes in the world are here, right?" I asked. Which about summed up my knowledge of Australian fauna.

"They rarely come in the back door," Grant said.

"Good to know," I said. "It's all strange to me. That I'm here, that you're my brother, my half-brother. It's hard to believe."

He leaned back, balancing his chair on two legs. "We'll just have to get used to it, won't we?"

Maybe, or maybe not, I thought. Maybe I should just get up and leave the heat and snakes, and monster bees and go back to New York right now. Had I expected some instant sense of belonging here? Or anywhere? Maybe this was just a bad idea from the get-go. I sipped my drink. I didn't want to be a coward. We had more vodka and I relaxed a little as we ate the cheese and they talked about Cameron.

"He was a surveyor in the outback," Grant said. "One of the earliest. Especially the Canning Stock Route."

"He knows the territory better than anyone," Jen said with obvious pride, twisting her ponytail around her finger. Apparently, she was still enthralled by stories of her grandfather as the legendary explorer despite Grant's description of him as a rogue. Or maybe because of it.

"When I was a kid, half the time we didn't know where he was," Grant said. "He broke my mother's heart long before he ever met your mother."

It had never occurred to me to think of my mother as the other woman, although that's what she'd been. Ida as femme fatale. I felt like I should apologize, but for what and to whom?

Jen touched her father's hand and brought it to her lips. It was startling to see such intimacy between father and daughter and I looked away, wondering how warm and firm his hand must feel, how enveloping. Outside, a hot wind tossed up bee-filled dust and the setting sun was red-yellow through the windows. I was uncomfortable, then uncomfortable with being uncomfortable.

"I take it you didn't follow in your father's footsteps," I said, trying to put my disquiet aside.

"I never cared much for the desert," he said. "I'm a naturalist, but I prefer swamps. And I teach."

Jen plucked an apple from the bowl in the centre of the table. "A *great* teacher."

Grant thanked her without embarrassment as I sat silent, unable to imagine where I might fit in here.

***

"Nice stroke." Grant stood alongside the hotel pool. Up since six and it wasn't yet seven, I leaned on the edge of the pool and pulled the cap away from my ears. Looming above me, he looked like a giant boy in rumpled khakis.

"What are you doing here so early?" I asked. We'd had an immense amount of alcohol the night before and planned to meet at noon when he would drive me out to Cameron's house.

Grant took off his baseball cap and shifted his weight from one leg to the other, so obviously ill at ease. "I thought maybe we could have some breakfast together," he said.

"No," I said and splashed water at him. "I'm kidding." I lifted myself out of the pool, not without effort. I wanted to keep swimming but towelled off and pulled on the hotel robe.

We sat at one of the tables with red-striped umbrellas and ordered coffee and fruit. The morning sun rising, already warm.

"Maybe I was unfair last night," he said. "About Cameron." He waited as though I might disagree.

"That he's never won father of the year didn't exactly surprise me," I said.

"You need to judge for yourself."

"I will," I said. "Doubt either of us would see him exactly the same."

Grant nodded, acting as if he wasn't sure why he'd come, which made two of us. We ate oranges and buttered rolls and commented on how hot it was, how hot it would be. He finished his coffee, wiped crumbs from his lap, and got up.

"Go on, finish your swim," he said. "I'll see you later." He looked at me like he was going to say something else but instead picked up his baseball cap, put it on, and walked away.

I watched him, long and loopy, as he pushed through the gate and disappeared. I had no idea what to make of him. I took off the robe, dove back in the pool and swam slow, easy laps.

Swimming was supreme isolation where only unforgiving memory followed me. Now, I thought of Stephen and the days he'd lose to what he called the flu and I called a hangover. How wrong I'd been in our early years together when I thought he was the exception in a family who drank like it was a full-time job; remembering the night at the dinner table when his mother, in a starched shirtwaist and Indian moccasins, leaned over and casually fell off her chair. No one said a word, including me, as she silently picked herself up off the Oriental rug, and it wasn't until years later that I realized my husband had joined the family business.

***

In the beginning, in Silver Lake, Stephen painted the giant abstract landscapes that would become his own while I worked in a downtown office to support us. There were days he didn't paint at all and I worried but excused it, thinking art couldn't be rushed. Our evening's entertainment was a walk around the block, the fall nights good and cold with crisp oak leaves under our feet and the burnt wood scent from neighbourhood fireplaces.

"There's so much to show you when we go to Paris," he said, never having been himself. He took my hand.

"I wonder when that will be," I said.

He kicked at the leaves and held on tighter. "We'll go."

It was a part of Stephen I loved. His absolute faith that life would take him, and by association, me, wherever we wanted. He believed in luck more than anyone I'd ever known. It was seductive, making me believe, too.

"You have to see Le Jardin des Plantes and the snakes," he said, as though Paris already belonged to him. "Montparnasse to see Baudelaire's grave, Jardin du Luxembourg."

Our luck held and we went in May when we were married two years, and he showed me all those things and more. From our hotel on the Left Bank, we sat cross-legged on the bed, eating croissants, jam sticking to the sheets, watching the bateau mouche on the river.

"I feel rich," I said, licking my fingers.

"Paris will do that to you," he said.

I trusted our life together would only get better.

"Did you know that you can tell how someone will make love by the way they dance?"

It was one of Stephen's theories he didn't think applied to him. He hated to dance. But now, in our Paris hotel room, he waltzed extravagantly across the room and pressed a button on the phone. We'd both studied French. I was afraid to speak, but Stephen talked to everyone, halting, yet eager, always learning. He ordered a bottle of champagne.

"It's morning," I whispered as if I could be overheard. "And we can't afford it." I kept track of our money, paid all the bills.

He said *merci* with a proper roll of the tongue and hung

up. "It's Paris," he said to me. "We can't afford not to."

It was so easy to give in and when the champagne arrived, we each drank a full glass and made love again. I fell asleep but woke not long after, startled and dizzy, slowly lifting my head. Stephen sat slouched in a silk chair by the window, the sun streaming in, the bottle resting on his knee.

"What are you doing?" I asked, softly.

"Drinking this champagne," he said. "I'm celebrating."

"Celebrating what?"

"Drinking this champagne."

It wasn't yet noon, and the bottle was empty. I told myself it was okay, after all, it was our first trip to Paris.

"We need to get out," I said. "Get some air."

"Fine." He put the bottle on the floor.

"I'll take a shower," I said, getting up. "We're going to the galleries, aren't we?"

"Absolutely," he said. "We'll see every brush stroke in Paris."

Minutes later, he joined me in the shower and took hold of the hand-held nozzle, playing, waving it wildly. "You must wash *la bouche*," he said, spraying water in my mouth.

He went on naming body parts using English with an elaborate French accent that kept me laughing, turning, and posing in the water. I pretended to be bothered as the water whipped between my legs and I grabbed the nozzle, turning it on him and he staggered, hugging me to keep the spray away and crying for mercy.

We left the hotel eagerly even as we tried to affect a

cool, European demeanour. I had on a linen dress and sandals. Stephen, sobered for now, with slicked-back hair and a white shirt. Not wanting to look like tourists, no sneakers, no cameras around our necks. Holding a cigarette would have added to what we thought of as the blasé continental, but neither of us smoked.

Stephen carried a dictionary but no street map. He had studied the city and knew where everything was and how to get there. All I had to do was follow. Down streets with shops filled with coloured jewels, books, bread, and pastries.

"There's a nice little Corot," Stephen said, stopping in front of a gallery.

I peered at the small seascape.

"He painted nature without idealizing it," he said, turning to me. "Why don't we buy it?"

"Yes, why don't we?" I started to walk away, but he moved to the door, pulling me along.

He's crazy, and I was with him. The gallery wasn't large. Pearl grey walls and the hush that comes with expensive things gathered in one place. A thin-lipped man with eyes the colour of the room came toward us, his hands cupped in front of his impeccably tailored coat, his mouth frozen, unsmiling. I stifled a laugh. Stephen poked me in the side.

"The price on the Corot?" Stephen asked.

The man looked from Stephen to me for signs of money: diamond rings, earrings, expensive leather.

"You're a collector?" The man asked.

"But of course," Stephen said.

I coughed and bit the inside of my cheek.

"We like to know where such things will reside," the man said, puffing out his bird-like chest. "You understand."

"How much?" Stephen asked, serious.

"Three hundred thousand." The man's lips barely parted with the words. "Dollars."

"Corot was the most forged of all painters," Stephen said, his nose close to the painting.

The man turned from pasty to white and a layer of perspiration appeared above his upper lip. He cleared his throat. "You don't think," he said. He looked dizzy, like he might faint.

Stephen plucked the card from between the man's clammy fingers and I held my breath until we were out the door and around the corner.

"Was it a fake?" I asked.

"Very possible," he said. "Corot produced a lot and that was a lesser-known work, the kind of thing forgers go for."

"Really," I said, continually impressed. We picked up our pace.

"Even over that prig's cologne, there was a slight scent of paint."

"Shouldn't we do something?" I asked. "Report him?"

"There's an unspoken tolerance for frauds in the art world," Stephen said. He took my arm. "Usually, the victims are too humiliated to speak up."

We walked, breathing in the smell of washed cement and baking bread, always bread, until we came to a café where we sat outside with a bottle of red wine. Stephen held his glass up to the afternoon sun.

"One day they'll be copying your work," I said. How

I trusted in his talent. "You just have to keep painting."

He poured the last of the bottle into his glass. "Right, that's all I have to do."

Five

Cameron's house was low-lying with a swath of untamed gardens, great piles of dying roses, fallen petals, leafy vines, and musty shrubs. The front door was slightly ajar. I'd invited myself, but he knew to expect me, so I knocked and pushed it open.

"I'm out here." His voice was strong.

I found my way through to a sunlit porch filled with potted plants and aging wicker furniture. Cameron sat on a cushioned chair surrounded by books and newspapers, coffee cups, and half-empty glasses. The air didn't move. He looked up from his paper.

"You're Lilly," he said, without smiling. He didn't look as old as I'd expected, plenty of grey hair, an oval face ending in a firm chin. I tried not to stare.

"You're my father," I answered. Did he expect me to run up and throw my arms around him?

"I didn't sleep last night," he said. "We should've put this off until tomorrow."

Really, well, I hadn't slept much either. Nevertheless, I'd been dressed and ready for hours, having changed my clothes three times. I had on a white skirt and tee-shirt, bright lipstick. My hair, washed and blown dry, shined. I was here to meet my father. And, he was tired? He'd had forty-five years to rest.

"I've travelled 14,000 miles," I said.

Resigned, he waved me in. "Come closer."

What about please? I didn't take orders well but moved further into the porch, which was screened all the way around and had dusty bits of leaves, twigs, and small bugs clinging to the outside baseboard.

"You could sit," he said. He adjusted his glasses, the wire frames tangling his hair, and squinted at me. His eyes were dark and deep-set like mine. He was clean-shaven and wore brown cotton pants with a freshly pressed white shirt. I wondered if he'd ironed it himself.

I sat, trying to act casual, failing. "I brought us some lunch," I said, holding the bag aloft like evidence at a trial. Where I came from food was the great leveller.

He nodded.

On the table beside him was a dog-eared copy of *Crossing the Dead Heart* and Bryson's *In a Sunburned Country*. In the corner, a bag of potting soil overflowed and the air smelled like things growing with the wet-dirt aroma of mulch made of leaves and straw. There were lacy ferns in cracked pots and velvet African violets and other spidery-looking plants I'd never seen before.

"You're tall," he said. "It's good to be tall."

"I didn't think so when I was a kid."

He pursed his lips like he was about to say something but didn't. Was he wondering how I had been then?

"I didn't expect to ever see you," he said.

"You never tried."

He didn't say anything. The air grew hotter. At one

end of the porch, an elderly grey and white cat sat cradled in an ancient swing hanging from the ceiling by a rusted chain. Frayed grass mats covered the floorboards.

"How could you not want to know about me?" I asked.

He snorted, a rough laugh, as if it was a joke, and placed his hands on his knees, stretching his fingers, his knuckles like hard knots. I softened, thinking of arthritis as he got up and took a few gliding steps, his worn loafers scratching the floor. He pulled at the wilted leaves of a plant, his back to me.

"I guess Ida told you everything," he said, turning with a shit-eating grin that gave me the creeps. Good teeth, I wondered if they were his. He sat back down.

"Not everything," I said. Almost nothing, really. Just the bare minimum.

Sunlight hit his face as he adjusted his chair. He was more weathered than old and he didn't have the blue-veined, brown-spotted pallor of old men. Instead, the Australian sun had cast him permanent walnut and I paled by comparison, like I'd just been born.

"You and your mother close?" he asked.

"Is that really any of your business?" The hair on the back of my neck was damp.

"Maybe not," he said.

There was a thick wall of air between us. I didn't know what I'd expected, but this wasn't it. I opened the bag of food. Have a little lunch and get the hell out of here. Long way to go for a turkey sandwich, but I'd made worse mistakes. How foolish to have expected anything more. Someone tender and welcoming, waiting for me, sorry for all the lost years, ashamed and repentant. Someone to be proud of, to be proud of me.

"Listen," I said. "There's absolutely no reason we have to care about each other." I handed him a sandwich. He looked at it and placed it in his lap.

"Pretty smart, aren't you?" he said.

"Enough to see you're only going to give me what you want." I leaned back, uncomfortable. Plant leaves curled in the heat. Why had he wanted to see me at all?

He scratched his chin and didn't look directly at me. "I don't have any money," he said, one eyebrow raised. "In case you thought you were getting lucky here. No opal mines, nothing like that."

I glared at him. "You bastard," I said, slowly, calmly.

"That would be you, wouldn't it?" he said.

I felt myself shake and looked around for something to throw, thinking how I wanted to hurt him. "You old fart," I said, through clenched teeth. "How could my mother ever have seen anything in you?"

A slight, obnoxious smile crossed his face. "You've got something of me in you," he said. A dry whiteness edged the corners of his mouth.

"I can't see anything I'd want," I said.

The cat stretched on the swing, it was way too hot for fur. I looked past Cameron outside where acacia trees, delicate as dreams, waited for a breeze.

"Calm yourself," he said. "I'm not that bad." He put both thumbs through his belt loops.

"Actually, I think you're just that bad," I said, pissed and impatient.

"I'm not making any apology for how I've lived my life," he said.

"Good," I said. "Because I'm not accepting any."

I'd had enough for one day. Maybe I was rash, but disappointment moved me and without another word, I got up and stomped through the house, letting myself out the same way I'd let myself in. Back down the front path, dried branches piercing the skin on my bare legs. Mad and miserable, I stood by the side of the road. Grant and Jen were due to get me in forty-five minutes. I didn't care, I wouldn't go back in. I would wait, sun beating on my head, dust filling my lungs, burning, hurting inside and out.

Cameron was rougher than a night in jail, as Stephen would say, never thinking it applied to him as well. My so-called father was a tough cookie, a cool customer, a piece of work. All the clichés fit him. Colourful perhaps, but I feared the reality was far darker and I didn't need another round with another difficult man. This wouldn't be one of those daughter-finds-long-lost-daddy stories ending in mutual admiration and affection. Cameron would remain a stranger. Unknown then and now. I didn't think there was any point in seeing him ever again.

Grant and Jen never asked why I'd waited outside, red-faced, nearly dead from the heat. Neither of them grilled me on my meeting, like they understood well enough. I supposed they'd both slammed a few doors themselves over the years. I liked Grant and I was thankful to Jennifer, but I planned to leave sooner than later. We'd keep in touch.

When I got back to my hotel room, the phone was

ringing.

"Bad start," Cameron said. "I'll be there in the morning."

It wasn't even close to an apology. He didn't ask if I wanted to see him again, didn't know I was about to pack up and bow out. I sat and stewed. He'd made the call, and I was a sap.

He was in the hotel lobby at ten, leaning against a pillar, newspaper under his arm. He wore tan corduroy pants, baggy sweater, and a troubled expression, as though uneasy in public places.

"We'll walk down by the river," he said.

I appreciated decisiveness. Herb, who I now thought of as my mother's dead husband, had been wishy-washy his whole life. Cameron gave orders, but okay, we'll walk. I was in a foul mood and hadn't slept. Maybe being by the water would help. I could always jump in. We crossed to a grassy park along the riverbank, sky blue and gold, people already out doing park things. We kept our distance, no light touch on the elbow, no familial arm in arm.

"Bet you didn't know Ida did the old Canning Route," he said. He looked at the ground, the river, not me.

Grant had told me that the Canning Stock Route, the toughest outback track in the country, was originally used to drive cattle from Halls Creek in the Kimberley region to Wiluna in the mid-west.

"I never even knew my mother had been to Australia," I said, calmed somewhat by the tranquilizing sound of water hitting the shore.

"She didn't want to go, but I encouraged her," he said.

"Turned out she was brave." He shook his head slowly as though surprised at the memory.

I had to remind myself he was talking about the same small, pastel woman living in an overly bright California condo. That he used the word brave to describe her.

"I want to know about her," I said. "What she was like then."

"There's time," he said.

No, there wasn't time. He was old, did he think he'd live forever? Families arrived at the park with baskets of food and too many children.

"Think you're up to going out there?" Cameron asked. "On the river?"

"The desert," he said. "Do what your mother did."

"Of course," I said too quickly. I wasn't even sure what he was talking about and I didn't want to go anywhere. I'd come all this way, wasn't that enough? Then again, if Ida could do it, so could I. I gave him a sideways glance. You old fart, I thought. It was a trick, a dare, and I'd bought it.

"No doubt, it would be my final trip," he said.

Sounded ominous to me. Maybe it was supposed to.

"It's a plan, then," he said. "I'll start putting it together."

We left each other on more or less better terms and the absurd idea that I would actually travel to the outback as my mother had done. I counted on it never really happening, that it was just tough-guy talk, and spent the day touring the city with Grant. Later that night, I stood on my hotel balcony watching boats on the Yarra River, the white trunks of gum trees barely visible along the bank. A familiar citrus smell floated up to me and I breathed deeply. I'd forgotten how scent could awaken memory, transporting you whether or not you wanted to go. The fragrance and the water reminding me again of Stephen.

***

The tropical air was sweet and mild the way night was supposed to be when you're on vacation. Stephen had decided to go for a swim after an evening spent drinking, and I sat in the dark watching as he did laps. The water shimmered under warm moonlight. I was tired, but I couldn't leave, afraid that with all the alcohol something might happen to him. I realized now that if he'd really wanted to scare himself, or me, he would have gone into the black ocean, but instead, he went just far enough to keep me on edge.

Sleek, broad shoulders rounded, he dove smooth and silent, alternating laps. Breaststroke, crawl, a length underwater. His skin shining, slick as a whaleback as he surfaced. My head ached from the wine. Stephen had finished a whole bottle by himself, which had become common for him. I thought of Paris and that long-ago morning champagne. I didn't know how he did it. Or how much longer he could. Could I? Years of raucous laughter turned mean. I loved him and he loved me. That's what we said. Still.

I felt myself whirl with the water as he swam lap after lap. Distracted by a group of waiters walking nearby, I looked away for a moment as they nodded at me then chattered into the dark. When I turned back, I couldn't see Stephen. Too long underwater. I stood up, straining, where was he? Surface, you fucker. He didn't. The water grew still and I moved closer to the edge, the pool lights made it hazy and difficult to see. Scared, I leaned over further, searching, ready to dive in when his head slowly rose out at my feet and he spit water onto my legs.

"Looking for something?" he asked, eyes red, lashes heavy.

"You think that's funny?" I yelled, relieved and furious.

He lolled back and took long strokes away from me.

"I do," he said.

"Scaring the shit out of me isn't funny."

He laughed, backstroking.

"I'm tired," I said. "I want to go to sleep."

"Go ahead."

"You could drown," I said, turning away.

Worn out and unhappy, why couldn't I ask him to get out, please? Please just come with me? Please hold me. That I was the one who was in danger of drowning.

Six

"I'm in," Grant said when he heard about the outback trip, and he convinced Jen to join us. I couldn't believe it was really happening and I was beyond grateful to them, knowing neither really wanted to go and that they were doing it for me.

I called Thomas in New York and gave him an update. "I'm going to the desert with my new relatives." He thought I was kidding. "Camping," I said. Thomas was still laughing when I hung up.

I needed some warm things, and a shopping trip with Jen would give us the opportunity to be alone.

"I know exactly what you want," she said, outside a store fraught with khaki.

"I thought you've never been," I said.

"True," she said. "Farthest out I've gone is the backyard, but I know what to wear."

I bought a warm shirt, two sweaters, and a jacket. We were done in twenty minutes and found a café in the sun. She looked at me over her double mocha latte with whipped cream.

"We could definitely hang," she said.

"I'll take that as a compliment," I said. At the next

table, three outrageously athletic men smiled at her. Obviously accustomed to the attention, she barely gave them a glance.

"You like my father, don't you?" she asked.

I hesitated. She was young and bright, and I thought there would never be a whole lot of anything that would get by her. I picked up my cup, tossed my hair back and tried to keep my brow from knotting or my voice from cracking.

"Of course, why wouldn't I?"

"Finding your brother, it must be astounding," she said.

"It is."

"Well, just so you know," she said. "He's pretty blown away, too. You've made quite the impression."

I didn't say anything because I didn't know what to say.

We only had a few days to prepare and Cameron spent the time with charts and lists while I worried about what I'd got myself into. This wasn't characteristic of me, taking off without a plan, trusting people I hardly knew. Sure, we're related, but that wasn't necessarily a good thing.

Finally, it was departure day. Dawn.

The four of us and our over-filled duffels headed for the airport. We took a commercial flight to Perth then changed planes. No time for sightseeing.

"That's it?" I asked, towering over what looked like an aircraft that came in a box. Small wouldn't describe it. Maybe tiny, maybe death trap.

"Don't worry," Grant said, nodding toward his father. "He's not the pilot."

"I could fly it if I had to," Cameron said.

Grant looked at me. "He could also walk on water if he had to."

"It starts," Jen said, tossing her pink dayglo bag inside. She climbed aboard.

I followed, wondering if I could I get out of this and thinking about Isak Dinesen and Beryl Markham flying around Africa. I'd always admired their stories. Adventuresome women from another time and place, I tried to imagine my mother, or myself, in their company.

Our pilot was from New Zealand, young and capable. It was a routine flight and I hated every minute of being tossed around in cloudless thermals, rattling gears, and nerves. Sunlight angled through the windows as we swayed and looped and finally levelled out. This was about all the adventure I needed and tried to pretend we were being airlifted out of Saigon at the end of the Vietnam War. I'd long been fascinated by the grainy footage of what appeared to be the ultimate escape. Enough for the images to remain forever in my head. Now, Grant leaned toward me, our knees hitting. When I dared to look out, the sky was layered in blue, dark to pale, then deeper again. The ground below wasn't the usual patchwork, no farmland grid or slice of road, just mountains of sand and ragged brush. Clouds hovered, shadowing the red earth. No one spoke. I gripped the hand rest and put on my brave face. Cameron looked at me with a half-grin and I knew he could see right through to my fear.

We miraculously landed safely in Wiluna, the town at the edge of desert where we were to pick up two

Land Cruisers and spend the night. Empty, dry and smoky brown, Wiluna had a nice far-away sound to it, I thought, like Jupiter or Mars.

"Where are we?" Jen asked, letting her bag fall from her shoulder.

It was getting dark fast with a few lights scattered on low, indistinct buildings.

"This was once the wildest town in Australia," Cameron said.

"Must have been a while ago," she said.

"There's only one bar left," he said.

"One is better than none. Lead the way," Grant said. And we followed our leader to the local tavern.

It was more like a hardware store that sold liquor. Bales of wire and rope were piled in the corner and implements hung by nails on rough plank walls. A row of dull light bulbs wired around a pipe ran the length of the ceiling, and a waist-high, glass-topped case filled with knives served as the bar so you could lean over your whiskey and ponder the weapons. There weren't any happy-hour accoutrements here: no bowls of nuts or chips, no cut limes or maraschino cherries. Above the bar in dusty splendour were several bottles with indecipherable labels and a sign that read, *Welcome to Paradise.* The kingdom of heaven held four other souls plus the barkeep. Saturday night, downtown Wiluna.

Grant got us beers and we sat around a barrel table. When we landed it had been at least 85 degrees, or 29 Celsius, which I still didn't understand; but now it was cold, having dropped to who-knows-what, and I hugged my jacket around me.

"Anyone going to wimp out, now's the time," Cameron said.

"Remind me why we're doing this," I said.

"See a place few ever will," he answered. "And to prove you're up to it." He looked at me, knowing I was a city girl.

I nodded, tried to look tough and show I wouldn't chicken out as he rolled open a well-used map. Jen looked over his shoulder, popping gum in his ear.

"That looks ancient," she said. "Are you sure it's accurate?"

"I drew it myself," he said.

"What about satellite tracking, GPS?" I asked. What century was he in?

"Get yourself good and lost depending on that stuff. Breaks down, you're dead. Stick to the old way, including the stars, and stay out of trouble."

My confidence in him increased only slightly. Maybe we wouldn't get lost and die in the desert. Maybe.

Grant, ignoring the map and his father, leaned back and sipped his beer. He smiled at me like he was the bad kid in school, his uneven features handsome in a rustic-gawky way. Cameron, head bowed, looked up over his wire glasses at us and I focussed back on the table.

"Everyone should know how to read this," he said.

My eyes glazed over. It was late, and I didn't drink beer.

"I can tell you right now," Jen said. "If we're lost, do *not* count on me."

"This is your grandfather's game," Grant said, pushing back his chair, he stood. "I do swamps."

"Fine by me," Cameron said, rolling up the map. "I'll handle it."

I followed Grant toward the door, noticing his shoulders, imagining the muscles beneath his shirt, thinking how an older, stronger brother protects his sister. The men at the other table tipped their glasses at us and Jen put her arm through mine as we headed outside to the local motel.

Half a dozen rooms, a cement path, brown exterior. Charming as a cave. The paper-thin walls of the room I shared with Jen smouldered under the dim overhead light. It was army-barracks functional with iron bedsteads and stiff, wool blankets.

She sat cross-legged on one of the twin beds wearing jeans and a bra, killer abs. "Did you notice those guys in the bar?"

"Not really," I said. I felt myself flush. I'd hardly been aware of anyone but Grant.

"I didn't think so," she said. She had on one of those sly, girly smiles and kept looking at me.

"What?" I asked.

"Oh, nothing," she said, like nothing was something she wasn't saying. "Did you like being married?"

"Sure," I said. "Until I didn't." Maybe, it wasn't marriage but the feeling of being trapped with Stephen on an ever-downward roller coaster.

"It's not for me," she said.

"You never know."

"I just want to have a lot of sex," she said, like she could shock me.

"A noble ambition."

Jen laughed. "If my mother had been anything like you maybe I'd miss her."

The cold came through the thin walls and I hurriedly put on pyjamas and socks. "What happened?" I asked, trying to be casual as I pulled back the blanket with my fingertips.

"She went on holiday one day, and never came back," she said without obvious emotion. "I was fifteen."

"Jeez, rough," I said, knowing it couldn't be that simple. Nothing ever was.

She shrugged. "I have my dad," she said, as though he was all she'd ever need.

It was cold and uncomfortable, and I couldn't sleep.

***

Our second time in Paris, we took a side trip to Giverny. It was only seventy kilometres, but we'd started late, it rained, and we got lost.

"Will they hold the room at the hotel?" I asked.

Stephen gripped the wheel, leaning forward to see through miniature wipers. "Monet, here we come." He made a fast right and eased onto a smooth highway. "I told the hotel it was our second honeymoon."

"Very funny," I said. "Since we never had a first."

"If you remember, it was right before my show at the temporary gallery. There wasn't time."

Or money, I thought.

We'd been married in our apartment with three friends in attendance, the ceremony performed by a mail-order Unitarian minister cousin of somebody. I'd worn a brown dress, long and shapeless, that looked wretched in the one and only photograph.

I stared out the car window at dismal French suburbs, nasty and grey and not one bit like The Umbrellas of Cherbourg.

Why hadn't I worn white? Brides always wore white, or ivory, maybe cream. No one wears a stupid brown dress. I'd tried for a non-traditional, arty look, but missed by a mile, although I didn't know it at the time. My brown hair hung in one of those Jane Fonda in *Klute* shag hairdos. We hadn't invited any family though they all lived close enough. Stephen didn't like mine, and I didn't like his. It worked out well in that respect.

"We don't seem like honeymooners," I said.

"We have to pretend," he said.

"How do we do that?"

"Just gaze into my eyes like I'm the best thing that ever happened to you," he said. "And I'll do the same."

Our wedding guests were a famous artist Stephen had studied with, who happened to be in town, a not-so-famous writer, and Sylvie, my best friend at the time, who kissed me, wished me luck and left, never to be seen again. Still, we were all smiling in that one picture, Stephen looking very much the bon vivant, as I recalled, champagne bottle in hand. Who knew it would become his trademark? I was in love and thought it was the best wedding anyone could ever want.

The rain let up, we made good time, and the sun came out just as we turned into the village.

"I figured the people at the hotel might put some wine in our room if they thought we were newlyweds," Stephen said.

"Very clever," I said.

Our hotel was a sombre building rescued by such lush gardens I thought I could've been looking at a Monet. White and mauve wisteria, yellow iris, and the purple delphiniums of spring. Every leaf shined from the rain. Stephen turned off the engine, the car still rattling as we got out. The air smelled new.

"This is good, but wait until you see Monet's place," he said, as if it was a friend's house and we'd been invited. "Too bad the water lilies don't show up until July." He slammed the car door. "Just means we'll have to come back."

Fine with me. It sounded good, anyway. And, so what if I hadn't worn white or never walked down the aisle, that there weren't any flowers or bridesmaids or music, no gifts of toasters and electric mixers. None of it mattered because I was convinced Stephen would be everything I'd ever want. I remembered now how good it felt to have that kind of trust.

Two elderly women stood on the hotel steps, wringing their hands in greeting. They were worried, they said, about our delay, that perhaps there'd been an accident. I put my arm through Stephen's and we smiled reassuringly.

Our room was small and filled with dark furniture. On the bureau, next to a bowl of fruit, was a bottle of red wine along with a note of congratulations.

"Admit it," Stephen said, opening the bottle. "I'm a genius." The cork popped.

I looked at my watch and checked the Giverny guide. "We can still make it for a short visit before closing," I said.

"Why rush?" He filled two glasses to the brim.

"Sunset, it would be so nice," I said. I didn't want to stay in and drink. I wanted to walk to Monet's house and watch the sunset over the famous gardens.

"There's tomorrow," he said.

I took my wine and sat on the bed. Resentful and moody like a teenager who'd been grounded, I slumped further into the pillows, increasingly sullen in the darkening room. Silently doubting my blind faith in tomorrow.

Seven

Daylight didn't do much for Wiluna. A grey town, the morning chill was thick with the smell of burning eucalyptus that added a layer of smoke to the dust. Curiosity had overtaken my questioning why I had agreed to this trip at all. Cameron leaned against a tree, wearing a bush hat, like a cowboy hat, only softer. He looked grim, all business.

"Good morning," I said, wrapping my arms around my body. If it was possible to nod grumpily, he did, barely looking at me as I walked over to Grant and Jen, who were stuffing the last of our gear into the cruisers. "Looks like enough to run a small country," I said.

"Need every bit of it," Cameron said, coming closer. He looked past Grant into the vehicle, checking how it was packed. "You've got some room on that other side."

Grant didn't pay any attention and kept packing.

"What happens if we get stuck out there?" I asked.

"Well, hopefully, we get unstuck," Cameron said.

Swell. There wasn't anything that made me think I was in for a good time, but I noticed something different in Cameron's expression I hadn't seen before. His eyes darted excitedly, and once he got behind the wheel, with his face flush from the cold and heading for the desert, he looked almost happy. He explained the complexity of our travel.

"Two vehicles are the absolute minimum," he said loudly over the noise of the engine. "People still break down and die out here."

I sat in the passenger's seat and stared straight ahead. "I appreciate knowing that."

"Everyone dies," he said. "This is as good a place as any."

I glanced at him, thinking it was more about time than place. Jen and Grant followed us in the other cruiser and we raced along the paved one-lane road until we hit the gutted dirt that marked the beginning of the famous Canning Track. It was an old stock route better suited to cattle than four oversized wheels. My neck soon grew weak from bouncing and my teeth hurt. I couldn't remember ever feeling so physically uncomfortable and thought it couldn't possibly go on like this, but it did. I tried to concentrate on the terrain, which didn't offer much beyond dried brush, though the sky, a wonderous clear azure, seemed to go on forever. We kept driving, not speaking and every once in a while, I'd catch Cameron looking at me.

"You remind me of your mother," he said, loud enough to be heard over the engine.

Happy for any conversation, I wondered what he saw in me. "We're very different," I said.

"That's what my son would say about me." He took one hand from the wheel and rubbed the back of his neck, staring intently at the road.

I looked at the ends of his hair curling along the crease below his ears and tried to imagine the young man he had been when my mother knew him. There was a softness and vulnerability in the nape of my father's neck.

Hours later when we finally stopped and got out, the wind covered us in a layer of grit. My whole body was stiff. Grant handed me a hot Coke.

"Having fun?" he asked, as though this entire manoeuvre was a joke I wasn't in on.

"I feel like I've walked here." I looked off into the distance, overwhelmed by the enormity of nothingness. "Wherever here is."

Saltbush spread over the desert floor, dry and shabby, like California sagebrush, along with wattles, wildflowers that were furry yellow and spiked, plus an occasional, stunted tree. Pure wilderness that I had to admit wasn't without a certain barren beauty.

Jen dropped an armload of tent parts at my feet. "Don't ask me," she said. "I have no idea."

We started to assemble one of two tents. It was close to dusk.

"Make the ropes tight or she'll blow away," Cameron yelled into the wind. Captain Bligh of the high sands.

The heavy rope dug into my hands, sweaty and dirty. I wanted to go home. Jen pulled and I tied, falling over each other as the sun set and a quick chill set in. The tent held steady, but none too inviting.

"How do we know where we are?" I asked.

"Stick with me," Cameron said as if we had another choice. "Got it in my head, plus the map and compass. We got all we need."

I thought what we needed were proper roads with signs and lights. I didn't know what I'd expected, but the night took me by surprise. It didn't just grow dark out here, it came on like a door slamming shut. What I imagined solitary would be like. I was afraid of everything I didn't know, which was everything. The threat of strange animals, bugs, and snakes, the darkness and silence. But I managed to keep my fears to myself.

Dinner helped. Grant grilled steaks, better than any I'd ever had in New York City. The wind died down, although it was still freezing, and we sat around the campfire like kids, the heat warming our faces while a hard chill clutched at our backs. Beyond the isolation, the cold, and the dark, the other thing I wasn't prepared for was the dirt. My hands were layered in grime.

"Will we ever get clean?" I asked.

"We'll rig a shower tomorrow," Cameron said.

"That should be lovely," Jen said, cleaning her hands with a baby wipe. "This is disgusting."

We had boxes of wipes and anti-bacterial soap. Why hadn't I thought about the lack of running water? Makeshift outdoor latrines? Me? I must have been out of my mind. How could I do this beyond a couple of days? How could my mother have done it at all? Meticulous Ida. Had she been so in love with Cameron that nothing else mattered? That she would follow him anywhere? Had I ever felt that way about anyone? In the firelight, Cameron's face appeared like the ridges of the desert track.

After dinner, he pulled out a deck of cards. I wasn't much for games. I always thought you could feel your life slipping away playing bridge.

"Count me out," I said. But he wasn't offering a game and I watched the cards flutter between his fingers as he shuffled with the dexterity of a pro and fanned out the deck face down. He looked at me.

"Pick a card," he said, confident and mischievous. "Remember it, then put it back in the deck."

I did. "A man with tricks up his sleeve," I said.

Jen chewed gum and tried tuning in the radio.

"Now reach into your pocket," he said.

I pulled out a card.

"Ace of diamonds," he said. Without looking up he put the card back in the pack.

He was right, of course.

He glanced at me. "There are certain rules in every game," he said.

I had no idea what he was talking about, but it didn't sound like it had anything to do with magic.

Grant had watched the trick with indifference. "Hope you're that nimble getting us over the sand dunes," he said.

Cameron's agility with cards made me think of Stephen and how effortlessly he'd taught technique to art students. I remembered the summer he'd been offered a teaching job in Napa Valley and I'd taken a leave of absence to go with him. We stayed in a small cottage. An idyllic respite, or so I'd thought.

Four o'clock, not quite cocktail hour, Stephen uncorked a bottle of red. "Not any good," he said.

He wasn't speaking of the wine, but his twenty students paying a high price for six weeks of classes with a working artist. A sometime-working artist, since Stephen had been holding a glass more often than a brush.

I tossed a salad, fresh greens from a local farm. "They're learning," I said, always trying for the hopeful note. I didn't want to be negative, didn't want to be the wife.

"You've either got it or you don't," he said. "They ain't got it."

I wondered if he thought he still had it. "Give them time," I said.

"There's maybe one girl," he said. "Lucy. Nice name, huh?"

"Unless she's a redhead," I said.

I followed him to the porch and tried not to notice how preoccupied he seemed or how the word girl stood out in my mind. I was young, too, but I wasn't a girl, maybe never a girl.

"There's still lots of daylight. Are you going to work before dinner?" I asked.

"Not in the mood." He poured more wine. "This isn't half bad," he said, reading the label. He held up his glass, peering through it to look at me. "I like your hair like that, very pretty."

I pulled on the ends and checked my reflection in the window, never quite trusting a compliment. "I thought your plan was to paint on the days you didn't have class," I said.

He didn't respond and picked up the bottle again. The summer didn't pan out as I'd hoped. Stephen, preoccupied, never painted and I grew restless, fearing trouble ahead.

Eight

The desert. Day one. Day two. I just need to get used to the drill: drive all day, hot, then hotter, then impossible. Stop. Have lunch. Tuna, bread, cheese. Warm Coke, warm juice. Oh, ice, I remember you. I love you, ice. Grant tells dumb jokes. "What did the bartender say to the hamburger? Sorry, we don't serve food here." I'm thinking he's the funniest guy in the desert. Cameron snarls. Jen blows bubble gum, reads Sartre. She's a mystery. We haven't seen another vehicle or human being. Sundown. Freezing. Campfire. Something grilled. Something canned. Thank god for wine.

"I've been wondering why you agreed to come on this trip," I said. It was the end of the day and Grant watched as I attempted to tie what I thought was a slipknot at the base of the tent.

"I couldn't let you go alone," he said. "Not with Cameron. Wouldn't wish that on any woman."

"I'm beginning to think you're not fond of your father."

He didn't say anything as we stood together in the last fragments of evening light. It would be dark in minutes and I'd begun to prepare for it. I tried to take in the lay of the land before it was lost so if I woke in the night and peered through the tent flap, I'd remember the sloping boulders weren't some frightening apparition. That was my plan, anyway.

"You knew about me, didn't you?" I asked.

"Cameron told me the day of my mother's funeral," Grant said, pulling apart the mess I'd made of the ropes. "The man's a genius at timing."

"So, you were curious," I said.

There was no change in his eyes, no smile or question about where I'd been all these years. Somehow, I thought the symmetry would appeal to him: that he had spent a good part of his life staying out of Cameron's way, while I'd come so far to get in it.

Grant stepped in front of me, his scent of cooling sweat strangely pleasant. "Let me show you how to do this," he said. He made a loop of the rope and slipped the ends through. "It's like a bowline for a boat."

"A good thing to know in the desert," I said. Surprising myself, I copied it perfectly.

"I'm sorry we didn't meet sooner," he said. "I could've saved you years of loose ends." He folded his arms across his chest and swayed slightly like he was waiting for something.

The sky turned navy blue with a scrap of pale grey and the last hint of orange on the horizon. I pulled on gloves.

"Cold?" he asked.

"Beyond," I said. "I admit I'm spoiled. I'm a fan of clean and warm."

Grant laughed. "Nothing wrong with that."

"Cameron would disagree."

"That's his job," he said. "Being disagreeable."

"Was there ever a time you two got along?"

He looked away. "A time." He wasn't going to add anything else and I wasn't going to ask. Not now. It was dark, just starlight and a slice of moon.

***

Third day, end of day, nearly sundown. We'd seen hordes of bugs and spiders, and two dead snakes, little else. "Outback mammals are mostly nocturnal," Grant explained. "They like to avoid heat stress."

"Making them a whole lot smarter than us," I said.

We sat outside the tents and I wondered what could get in. Had we tied the ropes tight enough? "Last night, I heard the sound of something I probably wouldn't want to meet face on," I said.

"Could be a small rat, but as far as animals go, there's not much to worry about," he said. "Unless you happen to get between a couple of big kangaroos, one cornered by another. They have a way of pounding each other with their hind feet."

I shuddered, still thinking about rats, small or not. The way I figured it, these creatures belonged here and I didn't. Grant filled my glass, the deep-fruit alcohol mixing with the layer of dust always in my throat. Best thing about this place so far was that I could drink and not get drunk, something to do with the heat and sweating it out, although a morning headache had become routine.

"Of course, I was curious about you," he said as if

we were still having the conversation from the day before. "But I couldn't imagine asking Cameron any questions." He wiped the back of his hand over his lips. "Although, for some reason, I knew when your birthday was, how old you were."

"I never got a card," I said. "That's a joke." Sort of.

"I had no idea what you'd been told."

"Or if," I said. We looked straight at each other, but I flinched first and studied my nails.

"I didn't think it was my place to find you or try to contact you," he said.

I scratched my leg, my arm, nervousness or some creepy crawling thing, or both. Grant didn't seem like a brother, half or otherwise. He lightly touched my hand.

"We'll figure it out," he said, holding my hand tighter, then letting go.

Nine

Not even a week, and I'd already started to lose track of
time. I checked my watch out of habit. We didn't have
to be anywhere except at the end of this desert, hopefully before my skin turned to leather. Bush flies showed
up each morning and followed us into the day. Thou-
sands. Waving them away was known as the outback
salute, and Grant told me Australians were accused of
mumbling in order to keep flies from entering their
mouths. There were ants and ant-like insects, which
were actually termites that build huge, tomb-shaped
mounds, plus there were scorpions that liked to hide
in shoes.

"Give your boots a shake in the morning," Grant said.

I was not cheerful.

When we stopped for the day, Cameron knelt down
and ran his hand over the ground. Rain and wind had
changed the track in the years since he'd been here. Gutted and pierced with no discernible pattern, it would be
easy to follow in any number of directions. Any number wrong.

"It all looks the same," I said.

"Not to me," he said, indicating the way with a lift of

his chin. He was confident, and, unlike the rest of us, he seemed more content the further out we went.

I wondered how I could be the child of such a man. When I first moved to New York, it took me days to figure out Fifth Avenue divided east from west. I remembered, too, driving out of London with Stephen, me acting as navigator, totally lost, caught in the roundabouts, laughing as the map billowed, filling the car. Until Stephen grew impatient, then mad, snapping at me.

We kept moving now. Though we weren't far from a place called Durba Springs, which had a promising sound to it, we wouldn't be making the detour. We had to cross two major deserts, the Gibson and the Great Sandy, as though one weren't enough. More than one hundred and fifty thousand square kilometres combined. Isolation and emptiness took over as comfort faded to memory. I thought about Ida and the tidiness of the house where I grew up. The two sets of kitchen curtains changed every other week, pressed crisp, the coolness of the stark living room, brown and pale yellow, where we rarely set foot. I wondered what she had been like when she was here. Daring, carefree? And, if that were true, what had changed her into the woman of that pristine household where it seemed insincerity had flowed from the taps.

Fifth night. It felt like forever. How far had we gone? How far to go? Except for the campfire, absolute darkness. And yet, I'd still strain to see into nothing. Cameron stood across from where I sat warming my hands by the fire. Just the two of us.

"I want to know about my mother," I said. "When she was here."

He took a step back. "She had a wonderful laugh."

I inhaled cold air, shivering. Did she? I couldn't remember the last time I'd heard her laugh.

"She was married, had a family," I said.

"I never thought to hurt anyone."

"No one ever does," I said.

"We were young," he said.

Young and foolish. I wasn't buying it.

"And then she was gone," he said.

It was so quiet you could hear a spider crawl. Cameron kept his eyes on the ground and I could almost feel the hard bones of his hands as he placed one over the other on his lap, a nearly inaudible sigh from his lips. I was angry and frustrated with his reticence. But anger wouldn't get me anywhere and I wanted him to keep talking. The fire snapped with falling shards and in the faint light, I could just make out Grant's face as he approached.

"It smells like rain," he said, coming closer. He looked at the sky and I looked at him, happy to see him, yet wishing he hadn't intruded.

"A quick storm," Cameron said. "Unseasonable this time of year."

It had never occurred to me that it would rain in the desert, but the wind picked up and there was a scampering of something unseen as clouds covered the stars and a light rain quickly turned heavy. We made a run for it, Grant holding my arm. I was overly conscious of his touch as I rushed to the tent I shared with Jen.

Cameron sauntered by as though he was waterproof, looking up at us from under his dripping hat.

The tent, so hot in the daytime, was now wonderfully comforting. As I padded around in heavy socks on the dry, tarp-covered floor, I thought of the rain-soaked streets of Paris. And Stephen. You're destined to remember forever the person you're with the first time you go to Paris. Years later, after we'd parted, I'd walked alone down the Rue de Buci when, in the distance, I instantly recognized his unmistakable walk. I moved closer to the stone building, lingering, watching him at the end of a long, cool block. The city became a blur in recalling the details of him: there was the slight shuffle of his gait, had it become more pronounced? Almost a limp, which he camouflaged with a studied grace. Slim, wearing Levi's, he carried something slung over his shoulder, a jacket? His head bowed, dark hair greying. I couldn't see if the green-grey of his eyes had paled or if his mouth still held the anticipatory smile, waiting for a laugh, a good story. I couldn't see his hands, didn't know what shoes he wore. I waited. Stephen rarely missed a thing, but he'd missed me. As he came closer, I hesitated, then turned my head and faded into the crowd. I haven't seen him since.

Now, the storm came in loud waves, and I climbed on my bedroll and opened the window flap to watch lightning flash. Each shock intensified with glorious white light against perfect black, and rain so hard I thought it might pierce the canvas. I'd never heard or seen anything like it. In the city, rainstorms always meant unavailable taxis and slate-grey clouds obscuring the high-rise summit. Here, it was extravagant, frighteningly beautiful, and calming. As if for the first time, I had a true sense of the force of nature. And, being a part of it, I was unafraid.

I scrunched deep down in my sleeping bag. Jen passed out hours ago on the other bedroll. My last thought before sleep took over was a vision of me walking between Cameron and Grant. We were all much younger and, on the edge, where I couldn't quite see, Cameron grasped unsuccessfully for the hand of a woman, her face indistinguishable.

I woke early, pulled on my boots, stepped from the tent, and sank mid-calf into the mud that was the morning landscape. The cruisers were stuck up to their radiators, Grant gunning one of the engines, wheels spinning and spurting mud in all directions.

"We should have crossed the creek bed before we made camp," he said. He smiled half-heartedly and turned his Demons cap around.

Cameron surveyed the mess, poking a stick into the mud. "It was too dark."

Grant kicked the gears. "We could have made it."

"Couldn't," Cameron said.

I wanted to cry as I high-stepped it through the muck. Jen appeared in pink pyjamas and boots, hands on her hips like she'd made a wrong turn at a slumber party. "What'll we do?"

"Get these beasts out, then figure how to get across," Cameron said.

The previously dry creek bed was now deep in mud that appeared impossible to drive through. Grant circled the cruiser and looked underneath, checking it out in that way men have that make women think they know what they're doing.

"Have to dig 'er out," Cameron said, stating the obvious.

Jen blinked, wide-eyed. I shivered and wondered why large, immovable objects were always referred to as female.

The sun came up pale yellow. Within an hour, the heat would settle in and now, with each of us at a tyre, we began to dig. I used to imagine myself on an archaeological expedition somewhere in Africa. Romantic, I thought, unearthing bits and pieces of the past. Well, here we were, far from glamourous, shovelling out this giant vehicle so we could get going. To where and for what? Cameron was happy tramping through the wilderness, and my mother, much to my disbelief, had found him enchanting. So now, I was following in her footsteps when all my life, I'd made it a point to go in the other direction. It grew hotter, and we soon peeled off our jackets and worked a solid hour until I thought I would just die right here. Why couldn't she have had an affair in Rome? I would have an Italian father who wore beautiful shoes.

We finally stopped digging and put branches under the tyres as Cameron got behind the wheel and Grant positioned himself against the rear. The cruiser inched slowly, a behemoth lifting from the ooze like some prehistoric being. We hitched the other vehicle and towed it out, then cleaned our boots. We set out again, and, for the moment it didn't matter how mud-caked I was,

I felt an inexplicable, overwhelming sense of accomplishment.

Cameron looked at me and tipped his hat back on his forehead with a slight smile. "You're looking more like your mother every day."

It was a compliment I wasn't sure I wanted.

Ten

We drove on, conversation dulled by the heat, and my mind wandered to Thomas in New York.

No doubt seated behind his mahogany desk in his grey flannel office, very buttoned down, very efficient. He might look out the window from thirty stories up and think about me, imagining me here.

But there was no way he could envision this vast, stony ground, the geometric pattern of dry, cracked claypans and the sense I had of being at the end of the earth. Or, maybe it was the beginning. Meanwhile, the rest of the troubled world went on without me as it always would. To be out of touch with the news of the day was unique for me, but not unpleasant. I'd read that it was better to travel hopefully than arrive, and I thought that was what I was doing, travelling hopefully. Reason enough to go anywhere. Even though I was unsure what it was I was hoping for.

I was in the passenger seat next to Cameron. "What else could you tell me about my mother back then?" I asked, my voice breaking the quiet. "Besides her laugh."

He raised his fingers to his lips and didn't say anything. He was the most taciturn man I'd ever encountered.

"Did you even care about her?" I wanted to push him, and I saw the muscles in his jaw move, like I'd hit a nerve.

"You're waiting for something you're not going to hear," he said, finally, concentrating on the road and seeming to end the conversation.

Did I want him to tell me he'd been in love with my mother? Well, it seemed he hadn't, and what difference would it make, anyway? What I really wanted was for him to care about me. And he couldn't do that either.

We came upon a stand of bloodwood trees and stopped. It was so welcoming to see this entire group, a form of eucalyptus, tossing in the wind. I hadn't realized how much I missed the sight of trees. Even in the city, there were grassy parks and trees bordered by flowers fenced in along the street; springtime was best with a great pop of colour that never failed to impress.

We gathered twigs and leaves from the eucalyptus and added them to our campfire for a sweet scent I thought might stay with me forever. Cameron pulled gear from the cruiser and pointed to the red-rock cliffs nearby. "There's a cave in there that used to have crystal water."

Jen grabbed her father's hand. "Let's go. I want to see it."

"You, too, Lilly," Grant said, with a nod toward the cave.

"It's narrow," Cameron said. "Watch yourselves."

The description and warning didn't make it very appealing, but Jen and Grant started in as I hesitated then caught up with them. The opening was broad with ample room to stand upright, but it soon narrowed and the ceiling lowered. Quickly overcome with claustrophobia, I felt my throat tighten. It was dark. I couldn't see Jen and Grant in front of me. Too silent, there wasn't enough air. I felt myself panic.

"I can't," I said, turning around, not sure anyone heard me. I hadn't gone far and once outside, relieved, limp with perspiration, I sat on a rock across from Cameron who was winding tent ropes in a neat pile. He didn't look up. "There are some things I just don't have to do," I said, rubbing my clammy hands down my pants.

"Your mother went right in," he said.

Good for her. "She was a lot younger when she was here," I said.

"That must be it," he said, not giving an inch.

Was it possible my mother had been more daring than I would ever be? I changed the subject. "Was this an Aborigine cave?" I asked.

"Everything was theirs," he said, gesturing to take in the entire desert.

"I'd like to meet some of them."

"It's not a pretty sight," he said. "They're broken."

"What do you mean?"

"By other people," he said, and now he looked at me.

The way we all break, I thought. He got up, and I watched his back as he walked with a smooth, easy gait, not quite John Wayne, but a definite amble. Without turning around, he pointed to the sky and a lone eagle floating high on thermals. Sky so clear it hurt.

"Wedged-tail," he said.

I looked up as the bird flew soundless in the fading light, then I stared at the cave, thinking about my mother and her bravery. Shit. I got up and made myself go back.

Five steps into the cave and the darkness surrounded me. I must be crazy but figured there was only one way in and out, so I had to reach Jen and Grant. I touched the rock on either side, expecting it to be wet, but it was warm and dry and I kept going, heard something rustle, thinking this would be a great place for snakes to get out of the sun.

"Grant?" I said his name softly as if he was standing next to me. I couldn't imagine my mother, little beige woman with earrings, doing this. Maybe Cameron was kidding. Some joke. Why would he do that? Why would I do this? I held my fear and kept walking. The space narrowed again.

"Jen?" Louder, echoing. Enough. I'd had enough. Just turn around. I did, although the tight passage made it difficult and the back of my hand scraped along the rocks, stinging. I licked my wound, sticky with fresh blood on my tongue. What was I trying to prove? Should have trusted my instincts and stayed put. Sweat collected between my legs and under my arms. The only sounds were mine. Rushed breath and footsteps crunching sand. I wiped my hand across my mouth again, tasting the blood-dust. How could I have missed them? I hadn't walked that far. Or had I? The entrance should be here. Right here. Not wanting to panic, re-membering another time. I'd walked up a closed stair-well in a downtown building to find the door locked, back down to the door behind me, locked. Trapped, scared, heart paining, until finally, someone opened the top door, sheer luck, freedom. Now, making my way through the cave, I slowed and stopped.

I'm not a dreamer, so this must be from memory: I'm very small, and there is sand, and water, and the taste of salt. It could be tears or maybe spray from the ocean. Someone has left me, so I think it must be tears. I hear my sisters laughing. There are wooden sticks, it could be a crib, but I'm not a baby, I sleep in a bed with flowers and a rainbow next to me. Salt splashes into my eyes, I'm tumbling, I hear loud voices, but I'm moving away until someone pulls at my arm and I'm lifted up and carried to my mother asleep in the sand.

I rubbed my arm, aching, as I started again further into the dark, listening for any sound, straining to see a faint light coming closer and then suddenly, yes, light, a torch. "Grant?" I said.

Silence. Nothing.

"I've got you," Cameron said, sternly, his grasp tight on my arm. "Come on." In minutes, we were out. "What the hell you think you're doing going in there alone?" He roughly let go of me, like I wasn't worth holding onto. "No one does that." He walked away, clearly pissed.

Chastised like a kid, I felt hot with humiliation. He hadn't called me a fool or a coward, but he didn't have to.

Grant and Jen never found the crystal water, and emerged from the cave at another, previously unknown exit. If Cameron hadn't come in after me, I would have been forced to just keep going. I thanked him. He replied with a rough grumble.

It was late now, colder, every word visible.

"You didn't have to go back in the cave," Grant said.

We sat alone by the campfire. Jen and Cameron had gone to bed early. The sky was black and cloudless, overflowing with stars more brilliant than I'd ever seen. The deep, endless night sky became increasingly comforting as I tried hopelessly to recall the constellations. All the names Stephen knew so well. How he would quiz me, how I would fail.

I was exhausted but still too unnerved to sleep. Instead, my hand cleaned and covered, I poured another glass of wine.

"I could be an alcoholic before the end of this trip," I said.

"So, what made you do it, go back in?"

"Sometimes, I think I'm more afraid of not doing something than I am of doing it." What I didn't want to talk about was my mother being more capable or that I could possibly be in unspoken competition with this woman I'd never before thought of as daring or mysterious.

Eleven

The weather was so intense that each day left little evidence of the one before. Rain turned to mud then turned to dry, caked gullies that appeared parched for years. I felt myself change as the desert stripped away at me, making me leaner and stronger, my arms and legs tanned to toast. In the mirror, I looked as I had years ago, older, certainly, but in some ways younger, too. Without the pigment of makeup, the natural colour of my eyes and lips became more distinct. My hair curled, the ends turned bronze.

Always thirsty, we drank water greedily and cautiously, mindful of our limited supply. Mixed with the dust in my throat, it was like swallowing sludge with a strong taste of minerals. The further we went, the more depressingly empty the landscape became. Lifted only occasionally by a shock of purple or yellow wildflowers in the miles of rocks and sand, the one lonely tree lost on the horizon as though left behind after some cataclysmic event.

We were somewhere mid-point in our journey when we reached the fuel pick-up. It was late afternoon, still warm but behind it, I felt the coming evening chill.

Cameron was in his tent mulling over the map while Jen attempted to wash her hair in the makeshift shower. Grant and I took off to walk around the nearby boulders, our steps perfectly paced.

"It's hard to believe you never came out here as a kid," I said.

"Nope, not until I was older, and then there was only one time and I'd forced myself to go," he said. "I foolishly thought it was a way to get closer to my father."

"It couldn't have been easy growing up with him."

"A genuine living legend," Grant said, tossing a stone across the sand. "But what the hell. Fuck him. I have my own life."

The desert was the rival that had taken his father. But Cameron had chosen it over his son, and it seemed Grant would never forgive him. And, why should he?

"What does a naturalist do?" I asked, looking at him from under my too-long bangs.

"I'm studying platypus," he said.

"Oh."

"It's fascinating stuff. Up at dawn. Muck around in swamps all day," he said with a wry grin.

I thought about cocktails at the Plaza, wondered what was on at Lincoln Center.

"Richard Leaky lectured to my college anthropology class," I said. "There was a time I thought I wanted to be Jane Goodall. Of course, everyone did."

"What happened?"

"Too impatient," I said.

He nodded like maybe that wasn't such a bad thing.

"I guess I just liked the idea of it, not the hard work,"

I said. "I wasn't the type to wait around for chimps to grow." I picked up a small smooth stone, tossed it from one hand to the other, and wondered again about his wife. What if she met up somewhere in the world with Stephen? I didn't know what made me think of things like that, but anything could happen. Look at me.

We stopped walking. The light faded fast and a brisk wind sent the sand swirling. Grant put his arm through mine, and I liked the way he held on to me. Brotherly. Sweet. Maybe. I pushed away crazy thoughts as we circled back to camp.

Cameron and Grant cleaned up after dinner, and I perched on a rock next to Jen, far enough away from camp so our tents glowed like lanterns in the desert. It was beautifully quiet except for the muted sound of metal dishes being tossed into a plastic box and a rumble of men's voices. I wondered what they had to say to each other that wasn't an argument.

"When was the last time you were in love?" Jen asked. She liked to come out of nowhere with stuff to throw at me. Her face was scrubbed, her hair long and straight under a knit hat.

"Swell question," I said. I didn't mind but didn't answer. "What about you?"

"Never," she said.

"And that guy you told me about?"

"Great sex," she said, proudly.

I kept quiet.

"I like him, but I'm not giving up my life for love."

"Is that what you think happens?" I asked.

"I think it sucks you in and takes over," she said.

I couldn't disagree with her.

"Cameron broke my grandmother's heart before I was even born, my mother broke my father's," she said. "Maybe it's in the blood."

The light nearly gone, I saw the outline of her straight nose, subtle chin, the edge of her smile. I jumped down and stood in front of her, put my hands on her shoulders.

"It's worth the risk," I said firmly. "Love. It is."

"Wasn't for my mother," she said.

Her mother had given up her own career to be a university wife. Then finally left. Why, and for what? Where was she? Was she happy? Happier? Jen said she didn't know and didn't care. Not caring was a hard sell, and I wasn't buying it.

"I'll never leave my father," she said. "Someone has to stick."

"You could lose yourself there, too," I said.

She looked at me as though the thought had never occurred to her.

Twelve

Another day. Not sure which one. The last drifts of cool air evaporated and the grey morning sky became an aching, brilliant blue. Sprawling dusty lilac saltbush grew alongside the track and here the sand ridges were more like waves, gently rolling. We drove for hours, chasing sunlight, and it was nearly dark when we approached the Aboriginal community of Moonara.

Hardly a town, there were a few scattered, ramshackle buildings made from rusted corrugated siding, a small corral without animals, and two trucks; one on blocks devoid of wheels, the other intact and seemingly held together by corrosion. Smoke spiralled from the buildings and added to the dry cocoa air, red-brown, like a sepia photograph only without the nostalgia. Aborigines, men and women, dressed in odds and ends, idled in front of an open-air, general-store-bar-gas-station. Dark skinned and dark eyed, they sat on straight-backed chairs or lounged on discarded car seats and sipped sodas as we slowly drove by.

We stopped, and Cameron got out. A muscled, copper-coloured man came forward. He had on a limp brown tee-shirt and army-green pants, which hung on him. He came closer, unsmiling, staring into the distance. His face was round and cherub-like with high cheekbones and a broad nose, he had abundant lips, and his hair was dark and curly. As Cameron approached, they avoided eye contact and didn't shake hands. The man gestured to a place we could make camp, and Cameron turned and climbed back in the cruiser. It was a brief and curious encounter. I waited for some explanation.

"People here live in their own world and they like it like that," he said.

"Don't we all," I said.

He gave me a so-you-want-to-make-something-of-it look. "Just stick close to camp around here," he said.

I wanted him to admit he'd screwed up. That he, too, had stayed in his own world and hadn't bothered about me.

After dinner, disregarding his own advice, Cameron headed for the town bar, and I sat by the campfire with Grant. I had piled on three sweaters and a jacket and could barely move my arms.

"Don't let him bore you with swamp talk," Jen said. Kissing her father's forehead, she walked toward the tent, ponytail waving in the dark.

I envied their relationship, or maybe I was jealous on some other level. I didn't know much about fathers and daughters. Whatever I'd learned I got from hanging around the backyards of friends or the family outing with someone else's family. At the beach, my friend's father twirled her around in the air, so joyful, so curious, and totally unknown to me. It was a whole part of childhood I knew nothing about.

Grant poured me a glass of wine. There was an uneasy restlessness about him I hadn't noticed before, his hands moving, a crossed leg swinging.

"I feel so far away from my real life," I said.

"Sometimes, it's hard to know which life is real." The fire hissed with the smell of roasted corn from dinner still in the air.

I thought of Stephen, missing the hopefulness we'd had. "What if you thought you were living your right life and you lost it?"

Grant hesitated. "If you're lucky, you get another one," he said. "Like cats."

He took a drink and shifted position. We sat close and he put his hand over mine. Friendly. Warm. Acknowledging, what? Our commonality? Our aloneness? It wasn't anything. Couldn't be. Wouldn't be.

"Lilly?" He moved his hand under my chin, lifting my face to him, and kissed me softly, then not so softly. And I liked it, tasting the wine on his lips, those full lips on mine, his arms surrounding me, silently demanding. His face so close I couldn't see him, the cold air warming between us. There was everything wrong about this except how good it felt. I was terrified, but not so much that I couldn't kiss him back.

A muffled scream came out of the night, and we let go of each other. More yelling, frightening on every imaginable level. Grant grabbed my hand and we ran toward the tent where Jen had retreated. He flashed the light on her, safely asleep, then followed the noise, louder now, coming from somewhere near main street, Aborigine town.

As we got closer to the squat building of the Moon-ara bar, we heard bottles and furniture crashing, the sound of voices grunting without distinct words. Grant didn't hesitate and slammed through the flimsy double doors. I was right behind him, and in the dim light, I saw Cameron pinned against the far wall by two men while others crowded around, yelling like fans at a prize fight. The room looked as I would have pictured a real American cowboy bar. Dark, lit only by two low-watt bare bulbs, everything the colour of dirt. A bucket, broom, and mop stood in a corner, obviously never used. Wooden chairs had been overturned, but the high table, used as the bar, remained standing, however precariously, on three legs with stones piled to serve as the fourth. There were maybe a dozen people, all with the same short build, the same unruly dark hair and black eyes that didn't look at us. A few women sat with their arms folded across their breasts, half-dozing in an alcohol haze.

The whole room was drunk. I stood motionless by the door taking it all in as Grant tore through the group, lashing out and grabbing hold of his father from behind while Cameron, fists up, punched air, fast-talking the Aborigines who seemed mystified by his sudden burst of energy. There was blood on Cameron's face and hands, but his eyes were steady, unafraid and fierce. Grant kept at it, pushing back and trying to clear a path to the door when the crowd suddenly grew quiet.

I couldn't tell who had been knocked out or simply fallen over drunk, but in the lull Grant quickly freed Cameron and I followed as he hurried him out the door and back to camp.

Jen, having heard the commotion, came out of the dark, pulling a down jacket over pyjamas. Ghostly in the flashlight, she squinted at us. "What happened?"

"A little tussle," Cameron said, rubbing his knee. He moved slowly and sat on a rock near the cold campfire. "It's nothing."

Grant, hands on his hips, stood over him. "They had you against the wall," he said, pissed off like a father with a son who'd fucked up.

"They wouldn't hurt me." Cameron had a fat lip, a cut above one eye. "Too much liquor, that's all."

Jen brought a wet cloth and the first aid kit. "There's like *four* people in a thousand miles and you get in a fight."

Cameron looked at her with his good eye. "Sorry kid," he said. "Didn't mean to wake you."

"And miss the fun?" She handed him a glass of water and a pill.

"What is it?" he asked.

"Take it," she said.

"You're crazy," Grant said, pacing in front of his father.

I was speechless, wondering about the possibility of an airlift out of here. This was our leader who we depended on, sitting on a rock, bleeding.

"I know these people," Cameron said.

"You know dick," Grant said.

I stifled a laugh.

Cameron looked up from under the wet compress. "I would've been fine without you."

"You would've been dead," Grant said.

"I can't die," he answered. "I don't have a will."

"You don't have anything anyone wants," Grant said.

Same thing I'd told Cameron on the day we met.

"Don't you two ever stop?" Jen asked. "I'm never having kids."

Cameron turned to his son. "I didn't know you had such a good right."

"There's a shit-load of stuff you don't know," Grant said.

Jen hooked her arm through Cameron's and walked him to the tent. Somehow, I had the strange feeling that Cameron had deliberately put himself in danger, but I had no idea why.

"Will he be okay?" I asked.

"He'll heal if that's what you mean," Grant said.

I thought of the kiss as Grant glanced at me. It had been so fast, surprising and not. I could pretend it never happened but that was impossible. Instead, I wanted to indulge in recalling every gesture, every move. His hands, rough from the desert, on my neck as he pulled me closer, as I didn't resist.

He's hardly my type. Or, so I thought. He hung out with platypus and I wasn't even sure what they were. Mammals, fish? Grant was raw, unpolished, and completely engaging; and I was on fast-forward, imagining my life with a scientist--my half-brother, shocking enough--slogging through swamps together. I'd leave New York and my job and to hell with convention, morality, and the rest. Then I stopped. Get a grip. It was only a kiss.

***

In the solitude of the desert, random memories came to me.

Tennis was our game. We played for years on weekends at the homes of wealthy where-are-they-now friends. Always in white, clean as spit. Stephen wearing shorts, Lacoste polo, me in the ever-popular pleated skirt. Doubles. "Hit and giggle tennis" he called it. But we played long and hard, pretenders to a life that was never ours.

I walked to the net. "I've had enough," I said.

"Never enough," Stephen answered.

It was time to stop. Everyone was chilled.

He stayed, standing alone at the far end of the court, practicing his serve as the rest of us pulled on sweaters and headed for the house. A half-hour later, he came in and quickly caught up then passed us on drinks.

When it was time to leave, we got in our old, second-hand, money-green Mercedes, Stephen at the wheel, picking up speed going downhill. Five minutes later, the flashing light in the rear view brought us to a stop. He walked the line, he breathed. He didn't stand a chance. He was going to the clinker, a short ride in the black and white.

"You can come and get him in a few hours," the officer said.

I did. It was nearly midnight. Stephen got in the car without a word. It was in the days you could buy your way out of a DUI. Over a thousand dollars we didn't have.

"There won't be a record," he said, as we drove home. "Like it never happened."

"It happened," I said.

Thirteen

We had planned to stay one night in Moonara, but in the morning, Cameron ran a fever and Grant decided we'd wait another day. Cameron remained stretched out on his bedroll, one hand draped dramatically over his forehead.

"There's nothing wrong with me," he said.

Debatable, I thought. And, as interested as I'd been in visiting the Aborigines, now I couldn't wait to leave. The bar fight had unnerved what little nerve I had. Although the people of Moonara remained subdued. No doubt sleeping off the gaiety of the night before.

Grant explained that this place was an outstation, one of hundreds in the Northern Territory, some with no more than twenty people. Indigenous Australians had been relocated from towns to outposts like this on traditional tribal lands. They might have a radio to the outside world. Might not. But they didn't need us. I'd never been superstitious and didn't know yin from yang, but the whole thing gave me the creeps. The desert was a hostile environment, and this was another world within it where we didn't belong. I counted on Cameron recouping by dinnertime so we could take off in the morning.

It was mid-afternoon. Hanging around bored, Jen had secured her hair at odd angles with a cluster of multi-coloured barrettes and was now absorbed in carefully applying lipstick the colour of cotton candy.

"You never know," she said, lifting a shoulder, posing. "Prince Charming could be just around the next ridge." She started in on turquoise eyeshadow.

"Trying for the kewpie-doll look?" I asked.

"Desert whore," she replied, tilting her head to get a better view in the hand mirror. She turned to Grant, playing with a soccer ball nearby. "Whataya think?"

He looked up. "Frightening," he said.

She pouted in mock dejection, dabbing blush on her cheeks.

God knows why anyone would bring a soccer ball to the desert, but I liked watching him, possessed with a grace I hadn't seen before as he moved quickly, kicking and slicing the ball from one leg to the other. In the tent, Cameron had finally succumbed to sleep. The air felt stuck. I slowly thumbed through one of Grant's books, "*Platypus, A Unique Mammal*," complete with illustrations. Flies buzzed. Just another afternoon at the end of the earth.

Grant finessed the ball further away, red clay lifting in the air.

Jen stood, her jeans rolled at the ankle, her shirt tied at the waist. "Doesn't anything ever *happen* here?" She spread her arms, addressing the sky.

"What did you expect?" I asked.

"Something mysterious," she said, eyelashes blinking with drama. "I like a little intrigue, don't you?"

"Maybe," I said.

"It's interesting, that under other circumstances, you and my father might make the perfect couple," she said.

"You're forgetting he's my brother. Half-brother," I said, feeling the heat, trying to act cool.

"No," she said. "I'm not."

She hadn't missed a move, even smarter than I thought. She shielded her eyes, watching her father who had skilfully kicked the soccer ball some distance from us. "What's he doing?"

I turned to see Grant who had stopped and now stood with one foot perched on the ball. Lost for a moment in a dusty cloud, he disappeared then appeared again as something moved behind him in the swirling haze of sand.

"Dingoes," Jen said, and immediately started toward him.

I could just make out four wild dogs and a pup. "They'll run away, won't they?" I asked, reluctantly following her.

We had come across dingoes before and they'd always scattered. More afraid of us than we were of them, Cameron said. Speak for yourself, I'd thought.

We walked fast, avoiding the needle-sharp spinifex shrubs blowing in the hot wind as we cautiously approached Grant.

"Stay back," he said. Two of the dingoes came closer to him, then retreated. "They're just hungry."

For what, I wondered as Jen reached into her pocket and came up with a packet of crackers, which she unwrapped, put on the ground, and took a step back. The dogs devoured it instantly, their red-ginger coats on fire in the sunset.

"Sweet," she said.

"What about that?" I asked, pointing to a fat, brown snake curling around the legs of the dingo pup. My first inclination was to run but quickly remembered not to. The rule was you're not supposed to run from bees or wild dogs threatened by snakes.

The older dingoes snarled, jumping and pawing the ground close to the snake.

"Don't move," Grant said. He picked up two sticks.

"What are you doing?" I whispered loudly.

"Just walk away, Dad," Jen said.

The dogs howled ferociously, pouncing as the pup whimpered, trying to free itself from the snake. A moment ago, I'd been afraid of the dingoes, but now, I watched in awe as they tried to save their offspring from the snake. My attention turned to Grant, who suddenly lunged at the snake, piercing the tail with one of the sticks and with a powerful blow, bashed its head with the other.

I jumped as blood and snake spurted across the dogs. They whined then quieted as a female moved in cautiously sniffing at the pup, making sure he was okay, then licking him away as the other dogs tore into the dead snake.

Jen did a little dance. "Dead snake, dead snake," she chanted.

Astounded, I looked sideways at Grant. "Have you ever killed a snake before?" I asked.

"Sure," he said. "All the time."

I knew he was messing with me, but maybe not. "That was amazing," I said.

Jen grabbed her father's arm. "You saved the pup."

"I once heard a story about some old guy who got bit by a snake and got so mad he bit it back." Grant wiped his brow with the back of his hand. "In this country people make up stories all the time."

"There's a lot of room out here. Guess you have to fill it up with something," I said.

"The need to tell stories goes back to the Aboriginal culture," Grant said. "It doesn't belong to us. Still, it's deep in the land, permeating us all."

"And now, we have our own true snake story," Jen said.

Yes, we do, I thought, marvelling how this small incident would become mine to tell and how it drew me closer to these two people and this strange place.

Fourteen

Trees without leaves or birds stood skeletal on the clear, golden, midday horizon. Grant drove one-handed, fumbling with the radio, his mouth set like a man on a mission. Strains of old Broadway show tunes came through the static. "The Hills are Alive" broke off, then picked up in the middle of "Getting to Know You."

"I hesitate to ask if we're there yet," Jen said, sprawled across the backseat and eating from a box of raisins. "We haven't seen fresh fruit in years. We'll probably get scurvy."

"Your grandfather says we're not far from Halls Creek," Grant said. The town at the northern end of the Canning Track was our outback destination.

Cameron drove ahead of us, alone in the other cruiser. Jen had offered to ride with him, but he'd waved her off. He'd been in a foul mood ever since being rescued from the bar fight by his son.

"What'll we win when we get there?" she asked.

"Hopefully a hot shower," I said.

"And the pure joy of having had this experience," Grant said.

We had come to an open-salt flat where it was easier to pick up speed, and Cameron suddenly took off.

"Where the hell is he going?" Grant said, leaning over the steering wheel, he gunned it to catch up with his father.

After driving so long on the gutted track, it felt good to move fast, and I opened the passenger window to let the hot air rush in, the sounds of "Oklahoma" crackling across this wide expanse of nothing. We pulled alongside Cameron, and Grant waved at him in an attempt to slow him down.

"What's the hurry?" Grant shouted across me and through the window.

Cameron held the wheel two-fisted, smiled his spooky smile, and blasted off.

Fast was good, too fast wasn't. And, this was way too fast for me. Jen gripped the bar above her. "Maybe you should have gone with him, Lilly," she yelled above the din. "I think he's pissed."

"Too bad," Grant said, hitting the gas.

Suddenly, it was a race. Father and son duelling across the sand. About as primitive as it gets. I pulled the seat belt tighter around me then gripped the edge of the leatherette seat with sweaty hands. I hated it when grown men did these things.

Grant pushed harder, so did Cameron, dust billowing between our two hulking vehicles. I closed my eyes against the sandstorm, picturing the carcass of twisted metal, us dead in the wreckage. Our own private doomsday out here in original Mad Max country.

"This is so stupid," Jen shouted.

"We're going to beat him." Grant's face shone.

I was scared yet fascinated. "To where?" I asked.

"The end," he said, focusing straight ahead.

Right. Wherever that fantastical end might be. This was obviously a competition far beyond being first, and it would be arrogant to think it had anything to do with me and why I was here. I was just an interloper and out of place. I looked down at my hands, rough and dirt-encrusted, unrecognizable. It would take a month of manicures to fix them. City girl thoughts as death in the desert loomed.

"Why don't you two just get out and draw swords?" Jen screamed.

It seemed longer, but it probably wasn't more than ten minutes when we abruptly hit rougher ground and slowed. We'd reached the end of the flat and stopped with Cameron seconds behind us. Grant got out, a controlled excitement in his eyes, looking suddenly taller as his father came around the cruiser.

"Good driving," Cameron said. He put his hand on his son's shoulder, an everyday gesture that didn't happen every day.

Grant had a half-smile as he got back in and slyly squeezed my hand. Still frightened but impressed by his driving and how much he loved to win, I watched him from the corner of my eye, wondering what I'd expected out here, pitted against the forces of nature and family. Did I think there'd be some grand awakening, something that would make me feel connected to Cameron? It hadn't happened. What happened was Grant, so complicated and beyond simple desire.

Fifteen

"I'm not going to ask you what you're thinking," Grant said, sitting beside me outside the tents.

"Good, I hate that question."

It was late in the evening after a hard day's ride, wind calm, and the lingering smell of charred wood and grilled onions from dinner. Jen and Cameron had taken flashlights, seeking creatures that appeared only in the early dark with pairs of green-glowing eyes.

Always cold, I wrapped a blanket over my shoulders and thought of the kiss, our kiss, and how we'd tried to avoid each other ever since.

"We've been circling," Grant said. He dug his boots in the sand, fiddled with the laces.

"With nowhere to go," I said. Heavily layered, I gestured clumsily beyond our camp.

"What if we'd met somewhere else?"

"Strangers," he said.

Not knowing what we knew, would the attraction be the same? Maybe. Maybe not. How much was I, were we, intrigued by the idea of transgression?

"We could pretend we're other people," Grant said. He picked up my hand. I felt a rush.

"Like we don't already do that," I said. My hand, both uncomfortable and easy in his. Hold tighter or pull away?

"Who do you pretend to be?" he asked like he cared. He moved closer, bringing his scent of lime and wool.

"A coward," I said, bravely.

He looked askance at me like he wasn't sure what I meant. Neither was I. Torn between the desire to be bold, to go it alone, and the need to be protected as the child I had been and would always be. But then, I could have said anything, and his response would have been the same: leaning into me, kissing the back of my neck, his breath in my ear, his hand gripping my leg under the blanket. Thomas once told me he thought all men were dogs. But Grant was something more, wasn't he? He wasn't just any man.

Here I was, now in my own brave new world. I didn't want to think, I just wanted to want. We got up and I followed him to his tent. I hadn't spoken another word. I didn't have to. The single lantern cast a spooky light on the canvas wall. Here was a place of men, steeped in the pungent alcohol of skin bracers and shaving creams, of leather and hard soap; the combination, along with the man himself, intoxicating.

Close together on the small bedroll, I moved my hand over the stiff fabric, then the cool of his pillow, the indentation still visible.

"Are we crazy?" I asked.

"Completely," he said.

His features softened and I smiled. Loving crazy, I moved to him. In some far corner of my mind, I wondered how long Jen and Cameron would be gone. Like adolescents, was it the exquisite danger of discovery that heightened our desire?

Grant took off his shirt. Then mine. I'd heard it said the best aphrodisiac was unfamiliar skin, and it was true. His arms around me, I ran my hands over his shoulders. Felt his muscles twitch. Fast naked, we climbed into the sleeping bag, looking at this man's body, hard and ready, red-gold hair in the half-light. My god, my brother. Incongruously, my smattering of French came back to me, *en famille*.

"Do crazy people care about right or wrong?" I asked.

"Does it matter?" His voice was satiny, eyelashes brushing my cheek.

Everything matters. Eventually. I knew that, but tonight, I was warm and I hadn't been warm in days. Swaddled together, our bodies grew hot and damp, the chill lingering on fingers and noses. I wrapped my feet around his, then up his calf, feeling the muscle, the wave of hair. This was just a moment, but hadn't I always believed in moments? I thought if you could string the sublime minutes together, you would have a happy life.

We kissed again harder, teeth touching, and moved quickly. As if hurrying would be our denial. I felt the soft callous of his hand down my side then solid between my legs. I quivered and let myself go, already gone. Compelled, by what? A kind of yearning, thrill-seeking. His mouth moved along my body. I wished I was drunk, but instead, I was clear-headed and thinking. What law or word broken. Without the fear of God, what was the terror I felt?

"It's all right," he said.

Of course, it wasn't. Grant lifted me further to him, urgent, his body in mine, wedded. A perfect family re-union. Breathtaking, hard biting, unable or unwilling to resist, moving together until exhausted, we released each other, already sorry.

I lay still, waiting for lightning to flash, for some ca-lamitous event. The wrath of nothing. The world didn't care. There'd be no hell to pay. Not now.

Grant got up and dressed in silence. I watched him. Cooled. We didn't speak, and I thought of my mother and Cameron in this same other world. Young and vul-nerable, how easily she must have fallen—in love? And could I, too, be falling in love with Grant? I wondered if Ida ever thought of heaven or hell and where I fit in. Was I the hidden disgrace or perhaps, the treasure? Hadn't she hoped her indiscretion would go unnoticed, and, never imagining the consequences, they'd simply said good-bye? The bill would come later.

I'd always hated the coming back, thinking the big questions that get hidden, pushed away in the midst of desire or lust, possibly boredom. Stephen. Again. He left. Got it? Abandoned was the word the lawyer had used, the word I never acknowledged. Or had we left each other? Gone, but still here. Now, I'd try to fool myself. Pretending, I'd put on my clothes and my cava-lier attitude and go on.

***

I hadn't expected to see Jen back in our tent, but she was on her bedroll, her legs stretched out in front of her. The smell of the heavy canvas mixed with lavender hand lotion and bug repellent creating our own comforting, moveable oasis.

"I thought you'd still be with Cameron," I said. "Looking for weird animals."

"Wasn't very interesting," she said. She concentrated on untangling a necklace and didn't look up. "Too cold, anyway." She held up the chain in the faint light of the lantern.

"Can I help you with that?"

"I don't think so," she said. Her voice had an edge. "You've been keeping warm?"

"We sat by the fire for a while," I said.

She looked up, eyes in a slow roll. "Don't you think it's totally creepy?"

"What is?" I took a breath.

"Jeez, you and my father," she said, looking away.

I sat on my bedroll and bit my lips, already rough from kissing. The tent was suddenly cold and stifling at the same time. I had to say something but couldn't. Jen would say everything I was afraid to tell myself.

"I'm sorry," I said, finally. No thought of denial or excuses.

"You're his sister," she said, with a hissing sound. "I know, half-sister, but still." She made a face.

"We never," I started, but couldn't go on.

"No one ever thought about me," she said. "That's for sure."

She was right.

"I wanted you to be my friend," she said.

She turned off the lantern and I was left in the dark,

silenced by her words. Like a cold slap, she'd said it all. This sweet and charming girl, my far-away niece I never knew existed. With one act, I'd changed the nature of whatever our friendship could have been. And, it mattered.

Sixteen

Exhaustion let me sleep, but when I woke it was still dark. Jen burrowed nearby. Nearly sick thinking about Grant, then Jen, I turned around in my sleeping bag and faced the tent wall. There was just enough morning moonlight through a crack in the canvas to see an insect with too many legs crawling in front of my eyes.

I slowly moved one body part at a time out into the cold and washed up with tepid water in a basin, what my mother called a whore's bath. Every two days, we'd rig a shower using a bag filled with heated water and a sprinkler head attached with a rope pull, hanging it from whatever we could find. For privacy, we formed a slight barrier fence with available tall sticks stuck into the sand and bound together with rope. It worked amazingly well, and I had to admit showering in the open air was a godsend I looked forward to like a prisoner waiting for reprieve.

Being an early riser must have been something I'd somehow inherited from Cameron. My mother and sisters were late sleepers, bathrobe women with cigarettes and coffee pots going into the day, although now they'd stopped smoking and ate soy, or talked about eating soy. I dressed hurriedly in nearly all of the seven articles of clothing I had with me, which I'd discovered was probably all I'd ever really need.

Cameron sat alone by the fire. Low moon lingering over his shoulder. A light bandage covered the wound above his eye, a remnant of the bar fight. He made fists with both hands then released them, stretching his fingers as if they hurt. I watched, wondering if Grant was still sleeping, as Cameron stood, put his hands on his hips, and bent side to side.

"You do that every morning?" I asked.

"No," he said. "Should."

His movements were precise as he took off in long strides around the campfire, his arms swinging purposefully, like an old engine warming up. He finished and sat down, poured coffee for both of us. I loved everything about coffee: the smell, the steam rising, the time it takes. I'd given it up more than once, but always came back. I wrapped my hands around the cup.

Cameron had on his standard Levi's and a mouse-coloured jacket, a navy-blue scarf at his neck. He was tall enough and tan enough to be the old guy in a magazine ad. When he was young he had to have been extraordinarily handsome, and I thought of Ida and how he must have looked to her. He hadn't said another word about her.

There was a hint of dawn in the sky and the stars began to fade. "Were you unhappy when you met my mother?" I asked.

"I didn't need to be." He was clear-eyed, perfectly still. "What about you?" he asked, wispy brows slightly arched. "Are you unhappy now?"

He'd never asked me much about myself, and the question had an icy edge I didn't expect. I was too busy judging him and my mother. Now, I felt exposed. My shoulders ached uncomfortably. I could act the innocent, but I wasn't. I realized I'd taken my own risks.

"Maybe we don't know why we do what we do," I said.

"That's the most ignorant excuse I ever heard. *I don't know.*" He repeated my words in a mocking tone. "Listen, for the most part, we just want to get lost," he said. "Be gone from our lives, no matter how good or bad."

Was that what I was doing? My thoughts of Grant and Cameron confused. The idea of getting lost, whether down unknown streets or swept away with passion, sounded so romantic. Nothing better. Other than being found. Hide and seek, didn't we all do it as children? Except Cameron never came looking. I thought I'd wanted to get mad and stay mad and blame him for everything wrong in my life. Instead, I wanted to ask him things that were none of my business.

"Were there others, besides my mother?" I asked. He didn't look at me. I wanted to know what kind of man he was. Or wasn't.

"How perfect are any of us?" he asked by way of reply. Like he had me all figured out.

I'd forgotten his ability to read the wind, to touch the ground and find his way. Did I really think he wouldn't see through to me and Grant? I could hold Cameron responsible for what he had or hadn't done to me, but not without admitting my own failures.

"We all make mistakes," I said. Some more recent than others, I thought.

"If you want to go on about it, knock yourself out," Cameron said.

He leaned back and stared up into the bluing sky. Smoke floated eucalyptus-sweet from the fire. I told him I wanted to know what made him capable of choosing to stay out of my life.

"There's not much to tell," he said

I'd travelled a long way to find out and wanted everything I could get.

***

The letter had been stuffed in with the rest of two weeks' worth of mail, he told me, piled where his wife always left it in the green glass bowl centred on the dining room table.

He hadn't bothered to take off his boots, covered with the usual coating of red clay. He'd ruffled the hair of their eight-year-old and sifted through the mail as he walked from the room, each footfall leaving a trail of fine sand.

His wife hadn't tried to hide that she'd opened the letter. It had a United States postmark, and she'd been curious. Cameron had never been a saint, and his wife was a patient woman, but she was also from strong Australian stock. For her, it was all very simple. Forget he'd ever received the letter, or she would leave for her family on the other side of the country and take their son with her.

"My choice was clear," Cameron said. "Lose my boy or to maybe know you."

"A rotten choice," I said.

Cameron had made the decision not to find me and yet, he regularly left his son for long stretches to go into the desert. I wondered if he still could have somehow tried to reach out to me. And, would he really have lost his boy? Kids could be hard to lose.

"Were you and your wife able to go on?" I asked. "Were you happy?"

"Not a chance," he said, suddenly aged, the lines around his mouth drawn deeper.

Choices everywhere. My mother and Cameron to have an affair, his choice to pretend I didn't exist, and hers to lie.

"You weren't the mistake," Cameron said. "Not telling you was."

Another choice. Like being terrified in a narrow cave where I never had to go in first place.

Seventeen

I drank more at dinner with each passing night, lingering at the fire and savouring the cold as some sort of penance. Cameron had wandered off to tinker with a piece of equipment and Grant buried himself in a book dedicated to action plans for saving marsupials and monotremes.

Jen had all of her clothes laid out in our tent when I walked in, hit by the strong smell of citronella meant to keep away mosquitoes, which I'd never seen, so it must work. We had remained polite, perhaps even understanding each other on a womanly level, no one older or wiser.

"What are you doing?" I asked. She'd put the lantern on top of three pillows so it would throw more light.

"Figuring out what to wear," she said, holding up a navy-blue tank top.

"For what?"

"Town?" she said. "Other human beings?"

We planned to be in Halls Creek in two days.

"Cameron says it's not much of a town. A few hundred people give or take," I said.

"One man I'm not related to will do just fine," she replied.

I let out a nervous laugh and got up, waiting for her to say something about her father and me. She held a raspberry red tee-shirt at her neck. "Gives a better glow, don't you think?"

I agreed, but it didn't matter what she wore. She was a knockout. I went outside again and circled the camp-site. The faint moonlight added to the surreal land-scape, boulders like beasts, trees like alien beings. Cam-eron was in the other tent, fooling with the short wave, swearing at it loudly. Another day had passed with me and Grant trying to act cool and now I shined my flash-light just beyond our camp where I saw him leaning against a lone tree, grey and ghostly, smoking.

"I didn't know you did that," I said, pointing at the cigarette.

"I don't. First one in years." He stamped it out with his boot. "Last one, forever." The smoke swirled around, casting him in an ethereal haze.

"How can you be so sure?"

"You shouldn't always have what you want just be-cause you want it," he said, with his now familiar un-wavering look.

I had my hands in my pockets to keep from reaching out for him. In that luminous cloud, he looked like someone from a dream or another world. When he leaned close to me, pulling me to him, I'd already lost all logic and reason, easily moved, his hands in my hair, kissing my neck, until he gently backed off, brushing my cheek with his fingers. He didn't say we couldn't go on, and I didn't say it was unfair. I turned away and left him, starting back to my tent, eyes on the ground, now colder than ever. When I looked up, I caught sight of Cameron standing nearby, caught by the light from the edge of my torch. I wondered how long he'd been there, if he'd seen us.

"You remind me of your mother, walking fast like that," he said.

We both knew how my mother walked, so what. I kept walking. "I'm going to sleep."

Cameron raised his voice. "It's not very smart what you're doing."

I stopped, the light pooled at my feet. "This from you?" I asked. I couldn't see his face and felt brave in the dark for the first time.

"You're only going to hurt yourself, trying to get back at me like this," he said.

I wanted to laugh. As though everything was about him and he cared whether I got hurt or not. "Don't go all fatherly on me," I said.

He snorted. "You just have to open your mouth, and I hear myself."

"I'm not like you," I said.

"And nothing like your mother, so you say." He tipped his head to the side, watching me. "You must have sprung from the ground, dropped from a tree."

"You're just nasty, aren't you?" I said. Maybe I didn't want to admit that I could be just as mean-spirited as both of them. My great inheritance. "I must have been crazy coming here."

"Your idea," he said.

"Not one of my best."

"Could have been worse," he said with a sly smile. "I could have told you not to come."

I walked away and stamped the red clay dirt from my boots. No thought of going to sleep, I sat near the tent in the sliver of moonlight and quietly felt myself panic. I'd been a model of indiscretion. For a moment, I envied my mother and the secret she'd kept. I felt exposed, wondering, wildly, if I'd wanted to be found out. Was there a difference between keeping a secret by lying, as she had, and hoarding the truth, the lie of omission?

The fire dimmed to a few red coals, both tents dark, everyone asleep. Something moved, silhouetted on the horizon. I flashed my light, too late. Probably a kangaroo we'd come across earlier. I'd learned to be still, no easy task, and put my feet on a rock, remembering the snake. But I grew restless and got up from the dying fire, thinking about Ida and the way she'd sounded when she told me about Cameron. Nothing matters, she'd said. At the time, I didn't know what she meant, caught up in her confession and myself. Now, I realized how different her manner had been. Bleak, pessimistic even. How her normally spotless condo had appeared in slight disarray. Maybe she'd really loved him. And he never felt the same. I shivered. I'd been out of touch with her for nearly three weeks. We'd always talked, even if we had nothing to say. Had she resorted to years of idle chatter because the real story was just too hard to tell?

I felt a pull on my sleeve and jumped.

"I didn't want to scare you," Grant said.

139

"Didn't work," I said. "I thought you'd gone to sleep."

"I tried," he said, rubbing his eyes with his fists like a kid.

If we had moved cautiously around each other in the days before we'd made love, in the days after, we'd slipped into other orbits. Now, he came closer with his sleep scent of well-washed flannel and after-dinner coffee covered by toothpaste.

I put my hand on his chest. "Cameron saw us together," I said.

"I don't care."

"I was thinking what we said about living our right lives," I said. "Wondering if my mother had been in love with him. If he'd loved her."

Grant raised an eyebrow and in the soft light, he looked exactly like his father. The thatch of heavy hair going grey, the same strong chin. "Cameron never loved anyone," he said.

Grant spoke with conviction, but I wondered if it was true. There was something he wasn't saying.

"He thinks I'm taking revenge against him," I said. Was I? It wasn't an attractive thought.

Grant passed his fingers lightly over his mouth, a gesture I recognized as my own. However different we were, there was a familiarity that drew me to him. He took my hand then let it go. I suddenly felt bereft, losing a part of myself I never knew existed. How could we let go of each other? But then how could we not? Shadows paled, the moon began to fade, and I pulled my jacket closer around me. What if the revenge had been his?

Eighteen

Animal tracks, like small craters on the surface of the moon, mysteriously appeared on the dunes. One more day, another night, and we'd reach Halls Creek. The air between us seemed combustible and I wasn't sure how we would make it without one of us exploding. With nowhere to go, we might as well have been locked in a room together. The transgression having taken up residence like the proverbial elephant.

We stopped often to remove spinifex clogging the exhaust, then drove along the base of the Breaden Hills, sheer ancient cliffs rising from the desert floor, and made camp at the end of a long valley. Conversation was polite, setting up, cooking dinner. There was an ancient well nearby where hundreds of chirping finches and budgies hovered around an old trough. In an odd way, I felt almost more a part of the family now, like a co-conspirator.

Cameron pointed out the seismic survey lines that led to nowhere. "People have died mistaking the track," he said.

I stared at the markings on the flat-bottomed gorge and thought about making good time on the wrong road.

"I am so over this desert," Jen said.

We were coming to the end, not far to go. I wrapped a blanket around me. "I'm looking forward to electricity," I said.

I couldn't get used to the black nights and the feeling of being unmoored, as if floating in space or dropped in the ocean. News of the outside world came to us sparingly through uncertain reception, but enough to know that desperation, death, and hunger continued unabated with every glorious dawn.

Jen poked at the coals of our last campfire and glanced at Cameron and Grant out of earshot near the vehicles. "What's going to happen?" she asked in a low voice. She didn't have to explain what she meant.

"Nothing," I said. "I'm going to go home."

Her eyes narrowed. She pointed the burnt stick at me. "How could you?" she asked.

How could I fuck her father or how could I leave? It was the closest she'd come to a statement of recrimination.

"You'll break each other's hearts," she said.

I wasn't sure our hearts had anything to do with it. Lust, or perhaps mild insanity. But Jen was young and romantic and, unimaginable as it seemed, she cared more about her father's feelings than she did about her own distaste at our involvement.

"I'm just going to go back to my life, to what I know."

"Was that possible?" she asked.

I didn't answer. The coals shifted, red-hot sparks floating.

***

The land beyond Breaden Hills became more pastoral, opening up to rural plains on our final approach to Halls Creek. Jen rode the last miles with Cameron, and I was with Grant, both of us worn out, silenced by the heat and engine noise. The weight of our intimacy as oppressive as the weather.

With the late afternoon sun at our backs, we pulled into the Edge Inn Motel. Peeling paint, run-down swimming pool filled with green water, a stretch of brown grass. Civilization of sorts. We planned to spend the night and fly out tomorrow, and I was already anxious about another flight in a small plane. As if there wasn't enough to fear right here on the ground.

The Edge Inn was far from anything and far from swell. Situated at the end of the runway of the local airstrip, noise would be minimal we were told, seeing as there was only one flight every two days. The idea of a room, any room, was overpowering. I couldn't wait to take off my clothes and burn them. I wanted to soak in a tub neck high with bubbles and cleanse myself from the desert, from everything.

I opened the door to a room painted a ferocious hot pink. The colour of bubble gum and 1957. Mouldings, doors, and window blinds were accented in shiny black, the bathroom walls a hard turquoise particular to lawn chairs. Scattered throughout were tropical mementos of some lifetime spent in port-side curio shops. Hawaiian dancers oscillated in ceramic pools and hibiscus clustered on ashtrays from Fiji. Dusty mirrors were encircled in plastic orchid leis. I felt as though I had walked into a fun-zone version of my childhood, all of it so horribly perfect.

There wasn't a tub. Instead, I took the longest, hottest shower of my life, then wrapped in a pink-striped towel, I stretched out on the bed like a giant Barbie-at-the-beach and fell into a deep sleep.

Awakened in the dark by a persistent knock, I had no idea of the time or precisely where I was.

"It's me," Grant said from the other side of the door, a thread of light at his feet.

Still in the towel, I opened the door to him leaning against the threshold, arm above his head, tempting. I wanted to pull him in, close the door, and forget again. I lightly kissed his brow. He smiled, looked me up and down.

"Nice outfit," he said.

I hitched the towel up my leg, vamping. He laughed. I loved to make a man laugh. Come on, once more, I didn't say, but he understood, walked in, and closed the door. I felt powerless or I wanted to think I felt powerless.

"We're meeting for dinner in half an hour," he said.

He sat on the bed. I took off the towel.

Out of the deep desert and surrounded now by these four ghastly walls, I understood that we would slowly descend back to earth, each to our own place in it, but we wouldn't go quietly. We held on, loving, defiant, lost.

After Grant left, I looked at my face in the flower-laden mirror and thought about my conversation with

Jen. Whatever lofty idea I'd had of myself, my great and noble resolve, had vanished in a moment of opportunism. I hadn't made it through a day.

Nineteen

I stopped at the sound of voices coming from the motel dining room and peered in.

Grant, visibly upset, paced the room, the veins of his neck protruding and his face red with anger. He looked hot as hell while Cameron sat with apparent calm, his legs resting on a chair. Their voices were strained in an effort to keep it down but rose nevertheless. I swallowed hard, leaned back out of view and stood still.

"Don't think you could ever fool me," Cameron said. "I know you up and down."

"Of all people to tell me *anything*," Grant said.

Cameron didn't take his eyes off his son. "You've got to leave her alone."

I held onto the door.

Grant's chin thrust forward. "Jealous, are you?"

My breath caught. Surely, they could hear my heart.

Cameron lowered his feet to the ground and leaned on his elbows, head down. "She's your *sister*," he said, slow and firm, spitting out the words.

Grant turned on his father, standing above and closing in on him until I thought he might strike. "And Kathryn was my wife."

I wanted to run but stood still. Kathryn. Grant's wife and Jen's mother.

"I gave my apologies on that score a long time ago," Cameron said.

I moved closer. The dining room was bleak, the odour of disinfectant overwhelming.

"Your apology never meant a thing to me," Grant said. His voice was low and raspy but still filled with venom. "I didn't kill you at the time for only one reason. But don't ever fool yourself thinking you're forgiven."

I took a step back, initially appalled they were arguing about me, but how presumptuous to think that's all this was. Jen had alluded to her mother's beauty and her boredom. Was it so hard to imagine what could have happened between Cameron and his daughter-in-law? The moment I thought it, I knew it was true. He was a scoundrel, but far worse than that.

And, me? I was his daughter.

Was it possible Jen didn't know? Had her father and grandfather kept the secret thinking they were protecting her? Stunned, I went back to my room to wait. For what, I didn't know. What I'd overheard was powerful information. But what would I do with it? When I finally left my room, I ran into Jen in the hallway, so clean she shined. I wanted to hold her.

"You look great," I said, stupidly.

"I took two showers and ran out of hot water," she said. "Now, I'm starving. Come eat with me."

I cautiously returned to the dining room with her. There were half a dozen tables in the too-big room decorated, such as it was, with dust coated plastic ivy in faux copper pots. Torn, outdoor carpeting covered the floors. I thought of Cameron's porch and the profusion of plants. Now, he sat peacefully across from Grant, beers in front of them, and no sign of their earlier argument.

"You two look cheerful," Jen said. She sat down and took a sip of her father's beer.

"Just tired," Grant said. He glanced blankly at me then looked away.

Cameron picked up the grease-stained menu. "Steak's supposed to be good here."

There was a smell of over-cooked onions, and I pictured a black skillet filled with an inch of old oil.

"Here's to survival of the fittest, if not the finest," Grant said, raising his bottle.

"Nobody hurt, we did okay," Cameron said, sliding the menu across the table.

An exaggeration on both points, I thought, wondering how I could I pretend not to know what I knew.

Flo, the manager-waitress, filled our scratched, plastic cups with warm water and stood patiently with her hand on her hip. She was blonde and blowsy, somewhere between forty and seventy with glistening green eyes looking for a way out. How did a woman wind up here? So far away from the world at large, and yet, perhaps no further than any of us. Maybe she'd been passing through and just got stuck. I thought about Kathryn, the runaway wife, wondering where she was, what she was doing and thinking, and how she could exist without her daughter in her life. In the same way Cameron had lived without me? And, my mother, was she also waiting, hoping to hear from me?

We gave our order and Flo returned with limp salad and bad news. Tomorrow's plane was delayed forty-eight hours. I'd never heard of a plane delayed for days.

"Happens," she said, tossing her hair back. "Fortunately, your rooms are still available."

What luck. Another couple of days here. No telling what else I might find out about this family. Grant and Cameron drank more beer, and I realized during dinner that I'd become a silent partner in their deception. How tempted I was to tell Cameron what I'd heard. Grant might be protecting his daughter with his silence. And, to be generous, maybe that's what Ida thought she'd done for me. But Cameron was only protecting himself.

"We've got two more days," Cameron said. "We can't just sit around."

"Why not?" Jen asked and I agreed.

"There's a natural pool somewhere around here," he said. "We should check it out."

Images of crocodiles and slithering snakes came to mind. "The last time we went looking for water was inside that cave," I said.

"It's just an old hole in the ground," he said. "Nothing dangerous."

I ignored him. The idea of trusting Cameron in any way was no longer an option.

"We could even do a copter flight out to the Bungle," he said.

"I'm not copter flying anywhere," I said.

"I'll go," Jen said. "I've read about it, huge domed-shaped massifs."

Cameron looked at Grant. "I'm sure you're not interested."

Grant picked up the last of his three beers and stood
uneasily. "Correct," he said, turning to Jen. "Just as
soon you stayed close by, too."

She started to protest then slumped back in her chair.
"No problem, I'll sleep."

Cameron twisted his mouth in obvious displeasure.
I'd wondered how Grant had kept from knocking out
his father at least a couple of times and realized now
why he didn't need to. He had Jen to use against him,
the one person Cameron really cared about.

Twenty

Morning came on like a headache. I opened my eyes in the fright room and rested my arm on my forehead already layered with perspiration. Above me, a fan slowly moved the hot air around and I thought about Thomas in New York. His rock-solid stability more appealing with each passing day. I'd found out all I needed to know here. This family was crazy, far beyond even my mother and sisters, and I was headed home. I pulled on shorts and a tee-shirt and wandered out to the broken concrete patio that ran the length of the motel.

"Morning," Grant said. He clutched a small rubber ball in the palm of his hand, working the muscles of his forearm.

I fell into a metal chair beside him, lifting my legs from the heat. He switched the ball to the other hand. Always messing with something. Give it a rest, I thought and leaned back, closing my eyes to the sun.

"It's strange you haven't asked me more about myself," he said.

"People usually tell you whatever they want to know."

"That's true," he said. "And who cares what your favourite colour is anyway."

"Black," I said.

"Absence of colour, figures."

"What *do* you care about?" I asked.

"Jen, and saving the platypus," he said.

I turned my head to look at him. "Are they endangered?" I asked.

"Which one?"

I rolled my eyes.

"They're more elusive than anything else," he said.

"No wonder you like them."

I had the feeling he wanted to tell me what I'd already figured out about his wife and Cameron. Maybe I could save him the trouble, but it was dangerous territory. If Grant had used me to get back at his father, I could be hurt and resentful, but what would be the point? And, what would it say about me and my own responsibility? I got up. "I need coffee," I said.

Something buzzed inside the dining room. I hoped it was just flies, always expecting to see a snake coiled in the corner, ready to lurch. Cameron sat hunched over a bowl of cereal and a yellowed newspaper. On the counter nearby, a scorched burner held a pot of mud coffee. I reached for a cup.

"It's poison," he said, not looking up.

I poured the coffee, wincing at the rank smell, added too much powdered creamer, and started to leave, sighing with the memory of early morning in the city and latte with fresh-milk foam.

"What's the rush?" He pushed his bowl away.

I stopped. Could I tell him I didn't want to be in the same room with him? That until yesterday, I thought he was just a cranky old man, a pain in the ass, at best eccentric. And now, he was so much less. It was an odd kind of relief. I found you, hooray for me, and now, you're someone I no longer want to know. Now, I can work on forgetting you.

"Looks like I missed the breakfast buffet," I said.

"There's another bowl, some cornflakes. Milk's not sour yet."

Unlike everything else around here, including me. I felt the sullenness in my face.

"You got something on your mind?" he asked.

He'd have to be blind not to see. I bit my lip, knowing I should bite my tongue. At any moment, I could reveal his nasty secret, smiling to myself, enjoying the power. I'm not so nice, either, am I? I leaned against the counter and looked down at my bare feet in urgent need of a pedicure. In this room of suffocating heat thick with lies, I suddenly felt free of any sense of decorum or restraint.

"You should come with me to the pools," Cameron said.

"I don't think so."

"Well, maybe Jen will change her mind and come along," he said.

"She needs sleep," I said.

"You're starting to sound like her mother."

"You mean Kathryn," I said sharply. Only Jen had ever mentioned her name to me.

He'd been leaning back and now he let the chair down slowly, fingertips gripping the table. The muscles in his neck tensed. The sound of her name surprised us both.

"I overheard you and Grant last night," I said, amazed at my boldness, my voice stronger than I would have imagined. "I know why she left."

There was a slight movement at the corner of his right eye, but he wouldn't look at me. "Jen doesn't *know*," he whispered.

"Of course, she doesn't," I said. "And you think she never will."

"You'd tell her?"

"And ruin the image she has of you?" I said. "That's all you're concerned about, isn't it?"

He didn't answer but looked up at me hard. I'd hit him where it hurt. My throat felt dry and I took a sip of bad coffee.

"And you and Grant, you care so much about her?" he asked.

I stared back at him, then turned and walked out.

***

I couldn't get away from Cameron fast enough, ducking back to my rotisserie room, thinking about Grant and his wife, then me and Stephen, and how hard it was to accept that we could be wrong about the people we fall in love with. I wondered, too, about betrayal and what part any of us played in our own deception. How culpable was the so-called victim? Something I'd never wanted to be. The dupe, the chump. I hated that role, which meant I had to admit my own participation, good or bad.

It seemed fair when I'd told Stephen I would take half the responsibility for whatever had gone wrong in our marriage. But no deal. *Everything,* he said, was my fault. This was right about the time he had all but stopped painting.

"I've lost it," he said.

"Did you ever think drinking might have something to do with it?"

"You just don't get it," he said.

"Because I'm not an artist," I said, although I was. Had been. Or could have been. Maybe.

"That's right," he said. "You're not."

"But Lucy is," I said. She was also someone petite and golden-haired, someone not me.

He didn't respond.

"You can't paint because you drink too much," I said. "And, you think screwing some young artist will bring it back."

I was mean, and I was right. But I didn't want to be either. I wanted him to love me. "You've seen her ever since Napa, haven't you?" I asked.

"She loves me," he said, with a demented grin he couldn't hold back. Like this was good news. Like I was his best friend, which I'd been, and should be happy for him. I wanted to know about her, this Lucy, hating myself for asking.

"How old is she?" Why was that important?

"Twenty-eight," he said.

I had to laugh, almost. I was calm and then not so calm. Dry-eyed, I threw things around our living room, mostly soft, nothing I really liked. He seemed to get a kick out of my anger, as though it was a compliment he'd been waiting for. That he was worth such rage. At that moment, I hated him, and myself, for what we'd become.

Calming down, I asked him if he still wanted to be married. Simple enough, but what about me? What if he turned to me regretful, begging and pleading?

"I don't know," he said.

Definitive as ever. Much later, I wondered if part my fury had been coupled with the idea that we'd both been sliding toward the same inevitability and he'd merely beaten me to the punch.

I had been the breadwinner, Stephen the artist. Instead of being the bored, unhappy housewife, I'd become the bored, unhappy working woman. Tempted by the smallest attention, how easily I, too, could have fallen, knowing now that betrayal was part of my heritage.

Twenty-one

I hung out sweltering in my room until past noon when the walls closed in, seeming to melt, hot and sticky. I hadn't had enough coffee and my head pounded. I checked out the dining room, quiet now except for the hum of electricity, and the patio where I'd left Grant was empty. There was no one around and for a minute I thought they'd all gone, somehow escaping without me, leaving me stranded. Or, maybe none of this was real and it was all some major cosmic mistake. Or dream. I felt slightly delirious, this endless heat and vast emptiness playing with my mind.

Grant said there was nothing normal about this country, and it felt somehow off-kilter. Far too much room here. It was getting on my nerves. People need to be crushed up against each other, I thought, longing again for New York and the comfort of crowds.

I looked out over the small burnt lawn and saw the dark figures of Jen and Grant in the distance. I wondered if he was telling her, but why would he and why now? I'd thought of my mother's reason, "because no one lives forever," as a sick compulsion to fess up. Although now, I'd probably be more charitable, recognizing her need to protect herself and thinking she was protecting me, too. I watched Jen and Grant until they saw me and we met halfway. He asked where I'd been as we started back across the lawn.

"I had a headache and missed breakfast."

"Be happy you skipped it," Jen said. She made a sour face. "They'd fry sand here if they could."

"We'll find someplace in town for lunch," Grant said. "Cameron took off early, going to look for those damn pools. Pure lunacy."

"At least he still loves to explore. That's kind of cool," Jen said.

Grant didn't respond, and the three of us got in the other cruiser for the short ride to Halls Creek main street in search of a meal. We passed pizza and hot-dog stands and Hon's Corner offering shrink-wrapped sandwiches until we came to Pearl Sands Chinese Cuisine. Chinese food at the end of the Australian outback. Seemed about right. We went in.

Pearl served us bowls of soup with noodles, explaining she was Hungarian with an affinity for Asian culture, having travelled the world for years with her now-dead husband. Another displaced woman. I wondered how she wound up here and why she stayed. I was curious, but not enough to ask. I had enough stories.

Jen poured tea. The red Formica table had been scrubbed clean except for the dark edge that ran along a metal strip. Soy sauce, maybe. I eyed it as though the heat would force the ooze out and onto our laps.

"How early did Cameron leave?" I asked.

"Right after breakfast," Grant said. "Peeled out like he knew where he was going."

"I thought he said you're not supposed to go any-where outside of town on your own."

"You're not."

I focused on the unidentifiable food Pearl placed in front of us. The smell of heavy pepper on what could be chicken and mushrooms floated in a grey-brown sauce along with something green threaded with red chilies. I spooned white rice on my plate, thought uneasily about my recent confrontation with Cameron.

"How far away are these pools?" I asked.

"No idea," Grant said. And didn't seem to care.

Pearl slid yellow plastic plates across the table at us. Nothing breakable was ever used around here.

"An old guy was here earlier, drinking whiskey, talk-ing about the pools," Pearl said, taking a step back and wiping her hands on her apron. "He said he hadn't been around here in a while. I tried giving him directions, but he wasn't having it." She reached over to another table for additional napkins. "Not bad looking either, but I'm over my limit."

I liked Pearl.

Jen put her fork down. "My grandfather wouldn't need directions to anywhere."

Pearl raised an eyebrow like she'd heard it all. "Well, could be he just wanted the drink."

I leaned across the table. "Maybe it wasn't Cameron," I said.

But we all knew it was. What we didn't know was why he would be in a Chinese restaurant drinking whiskey at eight in the morning. I thought of Stephen ordering a gin for breakfast "to quiet his stomach." But a drunk was just about the only rotten thing Cameron wasn't.

"I'll take you both back," Grant said. "Then drive out and have a look around."

"Not without me," Jen said.

"Without you," Grant said.

"What about the not going anywhere alone rule?" I asked.

He stood up. "I'm breaking it."

I wanted to go with him, too, but kept quiet. After our stomach crucifying lunch, he left us off to roast again at the Edge Inn. Jen flipped through an heirloom issue of *Vogue*, while I made an attempt at self-pedicure. A tired, half-dingo dog wandered over to our slice of shade, turned a tired circle, flopped down, and rolled over, feet in the air. The scene reminded me of old Booth cartoons in the *New Yorker*, and I tried to think of the caption.

"I don't get why we couldn't go," Jen said.

"I'm sure he had his reasons," I said, not sure at all.

She tossed the magazine to the ground. "I'm bored senseless."

"Only one more day and we're out of here," I said.

"You're ready too, aren't you?" she asked. "I guess the thrill is gone."

I wondered which thrill she was referring to. But, yes, I was over it. I wanted my own lacklustre life back. "It hasn't been dull," I said.

"That's like saying your friend's ugly baby has an interesting face," she said.

I smiled, swatting at flies on my arm, and wiped the sweat from behind my neck.

"What do you think is wrong with us?" she asked. "Aside from the obvious."

"What do you mean, wrong?"

"This family. Ever have the feeling you're a part of it but not?" She stopped. "Oh, geez, what am I talking about? They lied to you forever."

Yeah. Different time, different circumstances, but she could be me. Would it help or hurt her if I told her what I knew?

"The truth's overrated," I said.

"I hear you." She stood up. "Let's get out of here, go find my dad and Cameron."

"How?'

"The manager, Flo. We'll borrow her pick-up." She walked toward the office. "She's not going anywhere." I followed her.

Flo tossed us the keys. "Watch the clutch. It slips."

"I've had my eye on this baby for two days," Jen said. Faded blue, the colour of Levi's after years of washing. "I just love trucks." She got behind the wheel.

I got in on the passenger side. The seats were covered in torn vinyl and duct tape, the rear-view mirror was splintered, side mirrors non-existent. It smelled like gasoline, mildew, and greasy fries. The vehicle had absorbed the essence of Flo and the Edge Inn.

We only had a vague idea of the direction, but I agreed moving was better than sitting still. Terminal claustrophobia had set in a long time ago. Strange, in all this wide-open space. We'll just check up on Grant checking up on Cameron, nothing wrong with that. I didn't want to think about my last words with Cameron and the threat Jen knew nothing about. I wanted the dreadful feeling I had to go away.

I flipped through the brochure I'd picked up in the motel office and studied the local map without a whole lot of points of interest. "Fun fact: Halls Creek was once the oasis of this whole region," I read.

"A real garden spot," Jen said.

"There's more than one pool around here," I said.

"And more than one fool."

I held the sticky brochure with my fingertips and turned the map around. "Head south."

Jen glanced at the cracked compass fortuitously affixed to the dashboard. "You can't run out for milk around here without a frigging compass." She looked over her shoulder and backed up, narrowly missing the corroded motel barbecue. Dust whirled and settled behind us. "Are we going to have to check every place?" she asked.

"There's no other way," I said.

We left, passing through town and following the map not more than eight kilometres to the first pool formed by a scant river flowing between two rock cliffs. No bigger than a large backyard swimming pool, it was surrounded by shrubs and thorny bushes which looked every bit like the American West. No one around, we took off again.

"Flo said there should be a two-way radio in here," I said, opening the glove compartment, empty except for a few dead spiders. I checked behind the seat. Nothing.

"I was just thinking about women like that manager, Flo, and Pearl at the restaurant," Jen said. She tilted her head, pursed her lips. "Both alone, as if they're leftover from another life."

"They could have kids or family somewhere," I said.

"Like my mother, who didn't have anywhere to go, except away," Jen said.

Kathryn. I kept quiet as the truck filled with the heat of the day.

We listened to the crushing sound of the tires on the blistering cracked asphalt. I tried not to think about the possibility of a flat and no radio. You didn't have to go far to feel the danger of being totally out of contact.

"She could come back," I said. "Your mom."

"Or, I could go find her," Jen said. "Like you found Cameron."

Yeah, I found him okay. We drove for an hour and checked out two more deserted pools. It was still oppressively hot, but the presence of naturally occurring water was encouraging, a sign of true life on earth. According to the brochure, every river or waterhole in the top third of this berserk country was home to crocodiles.

"Your first encounter may be your last." I read on. "If it's wet, it's got crocs." I shifted my sandaled feet among scraps of Kleenex and newspaper on the truck floor, as if I expected some killer reptile to poke out from under the seat. "Knowing Cameron, he probably went for a swim."

"He's not stupid," Jen said. She made a sharp turn and I slid closer to her on the bench seat, righted myself.

We followed directions and passed a jagged limestone ridge called China Wall and continued on to Sawpit Gorge.

"Sounds like a place he would go," I said. "A pit."

The gorge had a fresh-water stream and gum trees all around and seemed like a good spot to camp if you had to, but it was also deserted.

"Not exactly a tourist attraction," I said. "There's just one more place to check."

"Maybe we missed him and he's already back at the motel," Jen said.

"Maybe."

It took another half hour to reach the tin gatehouse on Nicholson Station, where Marella Gorge, described as picturesque with deep, shaded pools, was located. Without any visible means of transportation, there appeared a grizzled gatekeeper, who might well have landed from Mars just so he could sit and tip his sweat-lined hat to the few souls who happened by.

"There's a job," Jen said, as we drove through.

"Strange, isn't it, this is the only place with a gate and someone to watch it," I said.

We passed through without a word and drove on until we came to the gorge, which opened to several pools surrounded by high grass and laced with hovering mosquitoes. Here the growth was deep, almost lush with the quality of an oasis, and I began to understand how Halls Creek got its earlier reputation. At the same instant, we both spotted our two cruisers on the far side of the second pool.

"Finally," Jen said. She turned sharply and made a fast stop, pulled the hand brake up with a hard jerk and we got out, slamming the doors. Parrots, roused by the sound, fluttered out of hiding and smoothly circled the water, flying in pairs, bright green, flecks of yellow and orange.

Jen looked relieved as we made our way single file along the fine sand bank. The mix of water, vegetation and heat made it feel more tropical than desert, although I knew we were west of true tropics. I bent down to touch the water, surprisingly cold, and rubbed the back of my neck.

"Cameron was right. The water does feel good," I said.

We walked on to the connecting pool, breezeless, nothing moved except insects dancing in the sunlight.

"I see him. I see my father," Jen said. Excited, she pointed to the far end of the pool and picked up the pace walking ahead of me to Grant, who was kneeling on the ground, holding a stick and drawing slow circles in the wet sand.

Always messing around, I thought, as the parrots returned, swooping low, afternoon sun golden on their wings. The air was dense with a musty smell of unknown life below our feet. I wished I had changed out of my sandals, expecting to see snakes or leeches or some other slithering thing that would wrap around my ankles. The idea nearly paralysed me.

Jen stopped abruptly, then moved closer, taking a few cautious steps. I was right behind her, trying to follow her gaze, when she quickly rushed forward. That's when I saw Cameron on the ground, stripped of his shirt, covered in mud and water, looking deflated as though the air had simply left his body. I didn't have to be told. I knew instantly that he was dead. He lay at his son's feet, and I couldn't help gasping loudly as Grant turned at Jen's approach, his expression half happy to see her and at the same time shock, or something like it, in his eyes.

"Dad." Jen rushed to her father.

Grant glanced at me and all I saw was profound, unforgiving anger move across his face.

Icy fear clutched at me. "My God," I said, letting out the breath I didn't know I was holding.

Afternoon clouds darkened the gorge and the air cooled. It seemed as if every living creature had been silenced.

Jen was momentarily speechless, the pink of her shorts, her sweet freshness in sharp contrast to the murkiness of the dank rock and heavy foliage surrounding us. Grant stood up and tried to put his arm around her, but she shrugged him away and got down on her knees, mud oozing into the sides of her sneakers, her hair hanging long over Cameron's motionless body.

"What happened?" She asked. Hushed at first, then frantic, she turned to her father. "How could this happen?" Her anguished voice, louder, guttural, pierced through the mud and stillness seemingly clear to the centre of the universe.

Grant threw the stick aside. "He was floating on the surface when I got here," he said, in a low voice, then turned his back.

I felt a shudder of fear and cold. Jen's boundless pain, my own stunned bewilderment.

"Damn fool," Grant said. "Water's ice, and the bottom of these shit holes changes all the time, no telling what the hell's down there." He looked at Jen again and rubbed his fingers over his mouth. "He knew that." He stared, dry-eyed, at the silent surface of the pool. "We'd been here before, together. I just remembered it now. A long time ago. He knew all about these places."

Jen's mouth hung open, her eyes moving from her grandfather's body to the water. "Maybe he was walking in and lost his footing." She needed an answer.

Grant shook his head and put his hand on her shoulder. "Dove in. The last thing anyone with an ounce of sense would do."

I stared at the body of the man who had been my father. Unknowable, lost so long ago. Now, lost and gone forever. No longer answerable. How would I grieve for him? For all the years or just for today and the impossible tomorrows? I felt empty, the way my mother said she felt after confessing to me. In the distance, the parrots called, then magically appeared overhead, fluttering gracefully into evening—still, the most beautiful and saddest time of day.

The logical explanation from Grant didn't alter my feeling that father and son, secrets simmering, had finally, disastrously come to blows. I saw the jagged gash on Cameron's temple, pink turning purple with hardly any blood. Because of the cold water, I thought.

Jen reached for her father's hand, and I stood apart as I always did and would. I thought of wounded animals that go off by themselves to die and how Cameron had been in a rush to get away. I felt myself shake, my stomach grab, wondering how seriously he'd taken my threat. I'd wanted to hurt him, but how deep had it gone?

We sat in a long silence until our legs grew stiff in the

late afternoon chill. No ambulance or coroner appeared to clean things up. Instead, we slowly lifted the body into one of the cruisers and left the other vehicles as we drove cautiously past the gatehouse. We didn't want to have to explain anything, and fortunately, the station manager was asleep, his hat covering his face. He could be dead, too. Would anyone even know?

The ride back to Halls Creek took a long time with Grant driving carefully, the way you would with a dead body. I turned to look at Cameron, laid out on the back seat, imagining him rapidly decomposing. I felt numb, but maybe that was just my way of excusing myself for not knowing how to act. Jen near him, her hand on his boot, her face streaked with dirt and tears. There was nothing to say and we didn't try.

We drove to the small emergency clinic in town where we filled out papers and put in a request to fly the body with us on tomorrow's plane. Pilots won't fly dead people without having all the details and we stared blankly, listening to the emergency staffer as he reeled off unwanted information. The clinic's one room had a high desk separating the business part from the medical, and beyond the desk where we stood were three curtained partitions, an oxygen tank and trays of supplies. There was a peeling Red Cross painted on the far wall and a strong scent of rubbing alcohol and bleach that made our eyes water, though nothing looked totally clean.

"More drowning from suicides than boating in this country, if you can believe that," the clerk said, sweat pouring from under his jet-black toupee. "Sign here." He looked up at us. "Not that I'm saying that's what happened, of course. Seems a perfect accident to me. Happens even to the best."

Despite his ultimate conclusion, it seemed he had other ideas but just couldn't be bothered to question us further. Then again, wouldn't someone have to weigh himself down in order to drown like that on purpose? Wasn't that something only a poet would do? More likely an accident, as the clerk said. Perfect or otherwise. Cameron hadn't known the depth and hit his head on the bottom, simple as that.

As we waded through more papers, I had the crazy thought of dressing up Cameron and buying him a seat just to avoid the bureaucracy. Maybe having such a macabre idea was only common to uncommon death. When we finally finished, we stumbled out into red dusk and silently made our way back to the Edge Inn where Flo greeted us with cold beer. Word had already got out.

We sat together in the dreary dining room made drearier by the presence of death seeping into us like the wind-swept sand. Grant laced his fingers around a bottle and Jen rested her chin on her arms folded on the table. Her eyes were red. She took a drink from Grant's beer and wiped her nose.

"Who are we going to complain about?" she asked with a half-smile.

I remembered thinking the same thing when I thought my mother was dying and wondered now what Cameron's death would mean to her. And what about Stephen, and how I'd always counted on the possibility we'd see each other again, and why that seemed so important. Being out of touch for years was one thing, but the idea of being lost from the world forever was overwhelming. I imagined we were all pretty much the same when it came to losing people and what it said about our own mortality. Scared to be gone, afraid of the infinite night.

Grant silently twirled the empty beer bottle, peeling off the label. I wanted to grab it away from him. I thought about what I'd said to Cameron, my guilt mixed with a sense of dark power. What if there had been another reason he'd never admitted anything to Jen about his involvement with her mother? Something bigger than his shame. What could that be but love? Maybe, he'd been madly, impossibly in love with Kathryn. Would that have made it any better? Was love everything? If not, what then?

"You can't go home yet, Lilly," Jen said, breaking the quiet. "You have to come back with us. Stay for the funeral."

I didn't say anything.

"Please," she added.

"Of course," I said, as though there'd never been a question.

Flo had outdone herself with dinner: roast beef not-overcooked, potatoes, and she'd found chives, sprinkled on Parmesan. "On the house," she said, placing the plates in front of us.

We ate because we were alive and hungry. After dinner, Jen took a Valium and went to sleep. Grant drank more beer and peeled more labels.

"Tell me what happened," he said.

I felt struck. "What do you mean?"

"Between you and Cameron." He leaned back. "The man never in his life took a drink before sundown." He moved his fingers over his lips, didn't take his eyes off me. "Something made him get liquored up and go out to a goddamned swimming hole, and dive the fuck in."

"What are you saying?" I asked.

"He didn't make a mistake, Lilly."

"A miscalculation," I said, shaking inside and out. "It happens. They said so at the clinic, even to the best."

"I thought suicide the moment I saw him," Grant said.

Suicide. I remembered what Cameron had said about this being his final trip, and the bar fight, the chances he'd taken. I couldn't look at Grant and focussed instead on a framed picture on the wall behind him. A photograph of a man and a small child that I hadn't noticed before, and wondered if it was Flo's family. Her husband was dead, but where was her boy, all grown up and disappeared?

"Tell me," Grant said.

I did. I told him everything, including how I'd threatened Cameron with telling Jen about him and her mother.

"I never would have," I said at the end, limp with regret.

Gone from Grant was the veneer of protective older brother, forbidden lover. "What was the point?" he asked.

I understood. Now. They'd had the situation under control, however skewed or warped I might have thought it.

"What would it mean if I admitted I liked the power?" I asked. "That it felt like I was getting back at him?"

"It would mean that you're part of the family," he said.

Perhaps. But now I was faced with the stark finality of death knowing I had lost forever any chance to acknowledge Cameron's own fragility. To take back my words, make it softer, or to say I was sorry.

Twenty-two

The authorities that managed the comings and goings of dead bodies wouldn't let us leave. A coroner was on his way from Darwin to verify and sign the death certificate. We'd be stuck here another twenty-four hours. Again, depending on flights out. My small, hot room felt like a jail cell and I was waiting for the governor to call. I tried deep breathing, thinking about New York out there like Xanadu.

It was late into the morning of our sentence, which threatened to be extended since we'd learned the coroner had been delayed. Wrecked, I went on the prowl for coffee and found Grant in the dining room, a heartstopping reminder of when Cameron sat in the same spot only two days before.

"Morning," I said.

He didn't look up and sat motionless, the chair leaning back on two legs, his feet balanced on the table edge, staring at nothing. I didn't know if he had ever really hated his father, but sustained hostility toward a dead person wasn't the same. It took the fire right out of it and changed everything.

"So hot," I said, for something to say.

He didn't answer. I picked up my cup and started to leave.

"Lilly."

I stopped, turned back to look at him, feeling a pull. Longing never ended on a dime. "What really made you come out here?" he asked.

My back was against the faux marble counter. "The chance to find out whatever I could about my father. And, my mother," I said. "What it was like for them."

Something sticky from god-knows-what shined on the countertop, and I moved my hand away. "It's hard to imagine our parents as individuals, young, in love or not, their passion."

He leaned back further, an impossible position with one arm draped over the chair, trying to appear nonchalant and looking uncomfortable. "And, what about us?"

"There's no us," I said.

"There was once," he said. "Twice, actually." Almost involuntarily, he reached for my hand.

I stirred. "A mistake," I said. "Both times."

His anger at me had seemingly been replaced, for whatever reason, with his need to hold on. Although, increasingly I had the feeling it wasn't about me at all and that I was a poor substitute for his missing wife.

"You told me you believed in moments, that there were no mistakes," he said.

"I was momentarily mistaken," I said.

He studied his fingers and I drank coffee. The clock on the wall had stopped. Yesterday? Thirty years ago?

I was being unfair. "You have to know, I also came on this trip because of you," I said.

He looked at me and now a smile stretched across his face. I felt myself wobble. So easy to fall.

"But it's history," I said.

"Recent enough," he said.

In the face of death, Grant's reaction to reach out to me again seemed normal and not unexpected, although I had this sudden picture of him as a brainy, slightly awkward, professor seducing moderately naive co-eds between platypus slideshows. And why not? What did I really know about him? Maybe he'd been the college degenerate and he was more like his father than not.

It was still morning, bright daylight, but this wasn't the desert with all its magical light and dark, all the mystery, freedom, and protective seclusion. We had come back to the world, a place with walls and electricity, running water, a place too close to home.

"Come on." He eased his chair down and offered his hand.

"I don't think so."

"Why not?" he asked

Plenty of reasons.

"It's not over," Grant said.

"Sometimes, the end just shows up, unannounced," I said.

He tilted his head. "You'll leave and be sorry."

"One way or another," I said.

I wanted to walk away from him, leave it at that, but hesitated. I needed to know if his interest in me, his desire, had just been a way to get back at his father for seducing Kathryn. I asked him flat out and waited.

He scratched his jaw, the light scruff of beard. "You Americans, always so bold," he said.

"Not always," I said. "But I'd like an answer."

"I understand," he said. "But you're wrong. Revenge never occurred to me. You sell yourself short, Lilly. I was as surprised about us as you were. You're a tough little cookie, for sure, but you're easy to care about."

I felt properly chagrined. After all, what more could I expect?

"Told you everything was strange down here," he said. "We're family, weird, but still family. Could we just leave it at that?"

I nodded. We could.

It was one o'clock and I was starving. Lunch was unavailable, and dinner would be steak and potatoes any way you wanted as long it was overcooked and fried. I longed for a green salad, fresh fruit, and sushi. I tried to imagine where Thomas was right now. Sweet Thomas, my safety net. At the moment, I wanted nothing more than a nice, boring dinner with him. I went into the deserted kitchen, opened the refrigerator, and stared at the congealed fat of last night's leftovers. Maybe I could rouse Jen and we could drive into town for something to eat.

I knocked softly. She opened the door, wearing a yellow sundress and carefully applied makeup that couldn't hide her puffy eyes. I smiled faintly. How many mornings had I, too, attempted the same camouflage? I wondered if there was a woman alive who hadn't spent more than one unending night in helpless tears. We like to think we're so strong, so powerful. Then the sun goes down. Her misery drew me in and I felt I would always want to know her, how she was, and where.

"Lunch?" I asked.

"Not hungry," she said.

"I'll eat for two." I held up the keys to the truck. "But I couldn't drive that thing to save my life."

"You could," she said. She grabbed her sunglasses.

We walked out and climbed into the truck.

"Pearl's?" I asked as if there was much choice.

She backed up, gears grinding into drive, and we took off, her ponytail bobbing in jolly defiance of her glumness. She liked driving so much it seemed to almost cheer her up.

It was a short and silent ride. I had a feeling Jen had probably figured it out about her mother and Cameron some time ago. That she'd had a sense of things gone wrong. But if she did know, it was something she'd keep to herself for as long as she wanted. The hardest part would be deciding who to hate, who to miss, or who to love no matter what. She could spend a lifetime working on that. Just like the rest of us.

Pearl handed us menus. "Poor devil sat right here drinking in the morning and by evening, the man's dead," she said, shaking her head. "Damn shame. But take it from me, fast is better. Lingering's pure hell. My opinion, go fast."

We ordered.

"Christ," Jen said after Pearl walked away.

"Tactful," I said. "Must be from living here."

"Or just living." Jen focussed on her hands folded demurely in front of her.

I sat back against the hard booth. "Most people just have difficulty knowing what to say."

She looked directly at me, challenging. "You want to

tell me what it is you know?"

I took a sip of tea. "Not really," I said.

She made a face. "You're all perfect shits," she said.

I swallowed, my brief moment of family euphoria faded fast. "Maybe you need to talk to your father," I said.

"Oh, right," she slumped back. "So, he could tell me what a rotten piece of crap my grandfather was."

I looked at her. "I don't think that's what he would say."

She leaned forward again. "Tell me what you know," she repeated.

I hesitated. "Probably not as much as you."

Pearl put two bowls of soup and another filled with rice on the table. She walked away without a word, like she smelled trouble. Jen picked up her spoon and slowly filled her bowl with rice. She kept filling it until the rice bowl was empty and the soup bowl overflowing. She picked up the hot mustard and spooned it into the soup, making a yellow muck. She looked at me, picked up the soy sauce, added it, and slid the mess over to me.

"I've fixed you some soup, Lilly." She smiled, sweetly menacing.

I stared at her. "You want to take it all out on me, go right ahead," I said.

"What do you care," she said, "You're leaving."

"Maybe it's none of your business what I care about," I said.

Pearl walked by, looked at the table and us, and kept going. Jen toyed with the spoon in front of her.

"They thought they were hiding it from me," she said. "What a joke." Smirking. "Kids always know what's going on."

"Some," I said.

She moved the goopy bowl away from me. "Sorry."

Pearl silently cleared the mess and brought us fresh bowls.

Jen tilted her head, appraising me. "Are you in love with my father?"

I looked away. "I guess I could be," I said, surprising myself.

"Too bad," she said.

"Right," I said.

"He had affairs," she said.

I nodded.

"Probably forever," she said.

I didn't say anything.

"My parents never fought," she said. "I think my mother hoped his cheating would just go away, like the flu."

"Still, it must have been difficult for you," I said.

She stretched her arms over her head. "I had an idyllic childhood for a while. Until she got fed up."

"And walked out?"

"That was later," she said. "After taking her revenge." She drew the word out, mockingly dramatic.

"You mean Cameron?"

She sat up straighter, serious now, and looked at me, challengingly. "What are you talking about?" she asked, smooth as cream.

"Same thing you are," I said.

Her face was expressionless except for a slight movement at the corner of her mouth. Then, suddenly agitated, she looked around the restaurant. "Can we get out of here?"

I glanced over at Pearl indiscreetly dawdling in the kitchen doorway. We paid the check and left.

Jen got behind the wheel.

"Where are we going?" I asked.

"Nowhere," she said.

We headed in the opposite direction from the motel. Jen, draping her left hand lazily over the steering wheel, her right on the gearshift. She was infinitely cool without trying and the most competent driver I'd ever known.

"My mother had an affair with Cameron out of spite," she said.

It was as if she'd literally needed to get out in the open to say it. Now, she gripped the wheel tightly and kept her eyes on the road.

I nodded. "How did you know?"

"Please," she said. "I knew." She paused then turned to look at me. "Just like I know about you and my father."

I stared out the window.

"Don't get all weird," she said.

"Maybe your mother created a situation so she was forced to leave. Even if she didn't want to."

"Maybe she loved Cameron," Jen said, defiant or hopeful, or both.

I smiled uneasily. "Falling in love might be the best worst joke the world plays on you," I said.

"You ought to know."

"We're talking about your mother," I said.

She looked askance and I knew what she was thinking. But passion wrapped up as love, still isn't love. Kathryn could have hated Cameron too, either because she felt she should or because loving him was impossible. I thought of Stephen, drinking, cheating, and still I cared. No wonder Kathryn left. Someone had to. Someone always had to.

Jen pulled the car over to the side of the road. There wasn't a sign or soul around.

"Did I ever tell you how beautiful my mother was?"

"You mentioned it." Did Kathryn's looks warrant her daughter's forgiveness?

"I told you I didn't miss her," she said. "I was lying." She held her hair away from her neck. I waited for her to say something else. "I pretend my father's a saint."

"Well, I guess we both know he isn't," I said.

She pulled on the door handle and we got out and walked, keeping our eyes on the ground. A hot breeze lifted the yellow-flowered wattle plants along the road, the sky achingly blue.

"I hated her for leaving," she said. "My dad hated himself more. He just wanted me to forgive him."

"And you did."

"I was fifteen. He was all I had."

"What about Cameron?"

"No one knew I'd figured it out about him and my mom. They had no idea how obvious it was, at least to me." She had an air of strength about her, though maybe she was trying too hard. "I've never said anything about it, never confronted them."

"Why not?"

"It was a rock in my pocket I wanted to hold on to."

"That could weigh you down after a while," I said,

though I knew how it felt to have that power.

"No shit." She picked a couple of vivid magenta wild-flowers.

I thought about my mother. "Your father said Cameron never loved anyone."

"My father's wrong." She pulled off the flower petals, letting them fly like wingless butterflies.

Jen saw it all clearly. For her mother, the affair with Cameron had been revenge against her philandering husband. But Cameron had fallen in love.

On an invisible signal, we turned around.

"What are you supposed to do when everyone in your life fucks up?" she asked.

We got into the truck. Slammed doors.

"Try to do better," I said. Except for the days you hide under the covers.

We drove back to town.

"Is it cocktail hour yet?" she asked.

"No idea." I'd stopped wearing my watch and told time by the weather instead. Chilly morning, hot day, freezing night. "Feels about 4:30," I said.

"God, you sound like Cameron."

I smiled out the window, missing him. But did I really? Yes. It was a fallacy to think I couldn't miss what I never had. Of course, I could. Not a father at all, Cameron had come in and out of my life in a matter of days, but did I mourn the man or the death of possibility? Of what I might have learned from him, about him, and myself.

We kept driving without much conversation.

Ever since the fight in Moonara, we'd steered clear

of the two bars in Halls Creek, but now Jen pulled in front of the cleverly named Creek Bar. The only other customer was bent over his drink and a butt-filled ashtray. He didn't look up. It seemed as though he hadn't looked up in very a long time. We ordered whiskey, which I never drank, but it fit the mood. Something to cut the dry dust and the crazy.

I took a slow sip. It was God-awful but warming. Jen didn't so much as grimace. This was a girl who hardly needed alcohol to embolden her.

"You're in love with my father," she said, flat out, and this time it wasn't a question.

"I never said that."

She held up her glass to the overhead light, peering into it with one eye. Something Grant would do.

"You said you could be. Same thing." She took a long drink. "He's still in love with her, you know."

"With your mother, not surprising. Abrupt departures will do that to you." I said.

"You never stood a chance," she said. Triumphant, she put her glass down.

I climbed up on my high horse. "It's fine. I'm not in love with him." In self-defence, resort to the truth, perhaps finally admitting it to myself. "Maybe I just liked the idea of it."

"Of the big, bad *taboo*," Jen said, emphasis on boo.

"That, maybe, and to aggravate your grandfather."

"Pretty shallow reason," she said.

I nodded. Yes, it was. I forced down another drink of whiskey. "I didn't say I was proud of myself." But I was leaving, and I thought she'd let it go with me.

"Do you think your mother will ever come back?" I

183

asked. Now that Cameron was dead.

"That's all my father lives for." She picked up her glass again. "Would you?"

I shook my head. "I'm not sure," I said. I'd always thought going backward was awkward.

Twenty-three

I noticed the morning differently only because it was our last. Though I felt like I'd been here for months, I also knew I had to actively take it in, seal it in my mind, and remember. There were things I thought would stay with me forever. The way the light at sunrise opened up the day, spine stretching like a giant book, the sky so brilliant it hurt, and Cameron, sifting sand through his fingers, reading invisible signs. I'd discovered there was freedom in being isolated and unconstrained by ordinary life. I'd learned, too, that my father was an imperfect man, and that I was as capable of bad behaviour as anyone.

Cameron's body had been zipped into a thick, plastic, ice-insulated bag and loaded on the plane as cargo. It was a gruesome endeavour and my dread of small aircraft only intensified knowing that one of the passengers was a corpse. We had to buy him a ticket, however, which I found comforting. Like he was still a person.

Death had been on my mind when I went to see my mother in California. But when I found out that Cameron was my father, wonder and excitement took over and my preoccupation with dying subsided. Until now, confronted with the sad reality.

I called Thomas when we landed in Darwin and told him about Cameron.

"The man spends his entire life in the desert. You show up and he dies?" Thomas said.

I stared down at the speckled linoleum, the air humid and flat. "Not exactly, Thomas. But thanks."

We changed planes for Melbourne, a long and solemn flight. I sat by the window next to Grant. Jen was across the aisle wearing earphones, drifting with the music. Almost without realizing it, I sleepily leaned into Grant until my head was nearly on his shoulder then abruptly sat upright.

"It's okay," he said, patting his shoulder.

"No, it isn't," I said. I'd forfeited the right to lean on him like an older brother.

"Figure out a way for it to be okay because we're not going to lose each other," he said. He turned to me and I couldn't help falling for it. Everything changes, but maybe he was right and it was possible for us to be in each other's lives.

Grant had arranged for someone from the funeral home to meet us at the airport and retrieve the body. It was a detail that had never occurred to me and I was amazed how efficiently bodies were whisked around the world like so many sacks of grain or mail. On our arrival, what remained of Cameron rode off in one direction as we walked out another.

***

The day of the funeral in Melbourne was perfect, the air fresh with early fall, our bright coloured scarves blowing in the wind. The green hills of the cemetery were a sharp contrast to where Cameron had spent most of his life. Maybe he would have preferred being buried in the desert, but he hadn't made plans to die. Or maybe he had. We'd never know. Certainly, he'd never written anything down. Probably because he'd never thought about his funeral and didn't care. He'd always been too interested in getting over the next sand dune.

I walked alone behind Jen and Grant, who held hands. They were true family. I was still and always, the outsider.

Funerals were supposed to help everyone through the first shattered days, but I hated the pageantry of public sorrow. Jackie Kennedy and those iconic images would always be the gold standard of funereal behaviour, a model of grief against which generations of women would measure themselves. Now, I, too, had the little black dress. The sunglasses. Pale lipstick. Hardly a debutante, yet it was my coming out party, meeting family friends. At the gravesite, Grant caught my eye with a look more of longing than loss, although maybe it was all the same. Jen, beside him, was the only one of us in tears.

Later, I stood in the doorway of Cameron's house, the lost and found daughter, as strangers came to pay their respects. I smiled at people I didn't know, who didn't know me. Better this way, they said. No suffering. How cavalier we were with other people's lives. Jen stayed close and together we passed around plates of roast beef stuffed into hard rolls. Grant held court on the patio, sitting in the same chair as Cameron the day we'd met.

Cameron had filled this room but now, all his papers and books had been cleared. Such quick work of a man's existence on earth. Grant, dressed uncomfortably in a black suit, his hair slicked back, moved his eyes from one person to another, shaking hands, easing into his new role.

It was early evening when the last guest finally left, and the house was quiet. There was the same orange-red sunset with the same bee-filled dust sweeping through the wild garden where I'd stormed out and away from my new now dead father. It seemed so long ago.

I leaned against the patio doorway while Grant rifled through records then got up and went into the house. It seemed he'd been looking for, and failed to find, something specific.

Jen slouched on the wicker swing, pushing it gently with one foot. A light breeze toyed with the dried leaves and bits of bugs against the outside screen. I wondered what had become of the grey and white cat.

"I've only been to one other funeral," she said. Scrubbed clean, without makeup, she looked fifteen.

"Who was it?" I asked.

"My best friend from high school," she said. Pulling a long strand of hair across her face, she examined the ends. "Hung herself in her mother's closet."

Shocked, I tried not to gasp. Jesus.

"She'd put towels over her mom's clothes so she wouldn't ruin them," Jen said.

A chill prickled my arms.

"Her mother had beautiful clothes."

I just stared at her in disbelief.

"It happened two weeks after my mom left," she said.

So much loss, poor Jen. And how lame I was, thinking I had her, or anyone else, figured out. None of us were that easy.

She kicked the swing harder as Grant returned with more documents in hand.

"We'll have to do something about this house," he said, looking at his daughter and avoiding me.

"Like what?" she asked.

"Sell it."

Jen gave him a piercing look but didn't respond. I wasn't a part of this conversation and didn't want to be. I wanted to pack my bags.

Grant threw a packet of papers onto the pile. "Just as he'd always said, he didn't leave a will. Even dead, he wanted to be as much trouble as possible."

Jen stopped swinging and stood up. Her face was red and her hands were tight fists. "Stop it." She didn't yell. Instead, she fiercely spit out the words. "It's not a fair fight anymore."

Grant, jaw twitching, leaned in and put his hand on her shoulder. "I'm sorry," he said. He looked over at me.

What did he expect? "We're all upset," I said. As if that was enough to explain it.

A sudden movement startled us as the missing cat walked across the patio and jumped onto the swing.

***

The days immediately after the funeral were the worst. With nothing pressing to keep us occupied, we spent the time drinking too much coffee and talking about the weather. Maybe we could have gone to a movie or out to dinner, but we stayed where we were, hanging around because it didn't seem right not to. When we spoke of Cameron, it was usually in reference to some annoying trait of his, which, not wishing to speak ill of the dead, we twisted so now it sounded as though he had been merely quirky or even amusing.

On the third day, the sky turned cannonball grey outside the guestroom in Cameron's house where I sat contemplating the call I had to make to my mother. Exhausted, the stark ice-blue walls added to my sense of chilly disconnection. I had been out of touch with her for nearly a month, but I couldn't put it off any longer and dialled her number.

I told her what had happened, or most of it, waiting as I heard her catch her breath, letting the news of Cameron's death sink in, trying to imagine what she must be thinking. How her heart might have fluttered, dangerously so, her mouth dry. Cameron had never been a part of the life she'd lived, but perhaps she'd seen in me a gesture, the lift of an eyebrow, or a certain cadence that reminded her of him. Memory so often just a flash, a sound, a divine moment of light.

"I always wondered if I'd ever see him again," she said.

Instead, it had been me to see him last and to witness his death. Not very fair. I didn't say anything and tried not to be impatient. I thought of myself and what if someone called to tell me Stephen had died. Haven't I, too, always imagined I'd see him again? It would be impossible to calculate the finality of it.

"How did he look?" she asked.

Startled back. "Dead or alive?" I asked, the words slipping out. I closed the door to the guestroom and sat in the amber glow of the bedside lamp.

"He was a nice-looking man, wasn't he?" she asked, ignoring my impudence. Did she want my approval of her choice?

I looked at my packed bags on the floor. "Yes, good-looking," I said. "Of course, he was old. Older."

"So handsome," she repeated, more to herself than me. "Dashing, really."

Yeah. A handsome shit. I thought of all I could say to her. Besides being a lousy father to his son, he'd cheated on his wife, flaked out on me, and screwed his daughter-in-law. And then, threatened, he cravenly offs himself in a fucking mud hole. That was your legendary, dashing explorer. But there was no reason to tell her. She wouldn't want to know. And, why should she? Leave her alone.

"Did you take any pictures?" she asked.

I imagined her smoothing her hands down her long sleeves, ordering her emotions.

"I forgot my camera," I said, which was true and unusual for me. I had a phone, but still not a shot taken. Then the battery died. All that scenery. But that's not what she was interested in. Naturally, she'd want a photo of Cameron. Not very considerate of me. I opened a nearby drawer. As if he was the type to keep a horde of pictures of himself.

"I'll try to find one for you," I said, looking at the boxes stacked between books and blankets on the closet shelf.

"That would be nice," she said. "Funny, I never had one. Just this picture in my head."

I waited. Was her image of Cameron as a colourful hero anymore inaccurate or selective than my own memories of Stephen? She'd hardly known Cameron and whatever he'd meant to her remained cemented in time, and maybe that wasn't a bad thing.

"I'm leaving soon," I said. "Coming home."

"Good," she said, her voice still small. "You're so far away."

"From what?" I asked, too sharply.

She didn't answer, but I knew what she was thinking. Like my living in New York, I was too far away from her. I softened. "Yes, I am, far away."

"I didn't think it was a good idea for you to go, but I didn't feel I could tell you."

I wouldn't have listened. I'd been pissed at my mother my whole life and never really knew why, some sense of wrongness I could never put my finger on. Still, the truth came out, maybe not in words, but in the silences and empty gestures impossible to hide. In the distance between us. As vast as two deserts. I understood now how deception could be more injurious than fact. She could have just told me.

Ida sighed. "But now, I'm glad you met him." She sounded tired.

We said goodbye and I hung up, strangely relieved. I thought I might find that my mother was someone totally different from the person I knew, a hidden personality she'd secreted away along with the information of my birth. But I was wrong. The accident of my conception was simply that, the cover-up was the true Ida.

I sat on the bed, thinking about her, old as she was, and Cameron dead, yet she still wanted a photograph, a memento. I checked the bureau and nightstands and pulled a chair over to reach the closet shelf. If I happened upon a batch of my old baby pictures up here, I'll just go out and shoot myself. My hands fumbled with a box above my head. I didn't want any after-death revelations, some secret journal where Cameron disclosed how much he missed and loved me. Fortunately, there was nothing.

Finally, I came across a black and white photograph taken about ten years ago when Cameron was truly handsome. And, yes, dashing. His face was smoother, his eyes brighter, but I recognized the same smirk, as if he'd just thought of a dirty joke, a wicked moment. I could see being attracted to him and, looking closer, I realized Cameron's younger face was exactly that of his son. It was like Grant staring back at me with that familiar devil-may-care expression that just sucks you right in. I had to smile at the idea of me and my mother, more alike than I ever would have thought, both flailing, falling.

I put the photo in my pocket. Maybe I'd make an extra copy, add it to my soppy collection as my mother would to hers. The irony was not lost on me. But I had to draw the line here. Even though it seemed I always preferred the broken line that let me pass, let me out, with Thomas, with Grant, even with Stephen. Still, it was nice to have a picture.

I sat, waiting for nothing until there was a light knock and I opened the door.

"Can I come in?" Grant said.

He sat near me on a corner of the bed. There was a scent of his lime aftershave that I'd come to know so well.

"I wanted you to know, I've just had a talk with Jen," he said, taking my hand. We went into the kitchen, Cameron's kitchen, where it seemed nothing had been cooked for a long time.

Jen stood at the stove, heat from multiple pots steaming the windows. She had on an extra-large Yankees tee-shirt, her hair a tangled bird's nest.

"Where did you get that?" I asked, pointing to the shirt.

"Old boyfriend." Chewing on a carrot, her face flushed. "I like the souvenirs of love, don't you?"

"Sure." My mind rustled through the boxes of photographs and letters I kept in New York, so sentimental. What did it mean and where would it all wind up? Like Cameron's papers and books, traces of who he was, cleared away.

Grant went out to get the mail and I watched him through the window, his walk more assured as he pulled at the weeds in his father's unruly garden. Jen slammed the oven door with a gloved hand.

"Chicken pot pie, roast beef, potatoes, and strawberry trifle," she said. "I started cooking and couldn't stop." She blew the hair away from her eyes. "So, we've had it out, my dad and me." She pulled off the gloves. "At least, he likes to think we have." She filled a plate of food and handed it to me.

I thanked her.

"Now, we know out loud what we've always known," she said.

Grant came in and Jen glanced at us both. I studied my plate and marvelled at how effortlessly they'd seemed to have reconciled. I was envious. They'd acknowledged the lie and adapted to the truth. I wondered if it would be possible for my mother and me to do the same.

Jen turned to me. "You're never coming back here, are you, Lilly?"

I looked at her uneasily. "Maybe you'll visit me." It sounded like a good idea whether it was or not. I wanted to try to do something for her and she brightened with new energy.

"Yes! New York. I want to shop everywhere, go to shows and museums."

Her enthusiasm was heartening, or heartbreaking. She was the best of us.

Grant watched me like he was waiting for me to say something else. "What?" I asked.

He held his hands open. "I'm not invited?"

"Sure, you are," I said, although somehow, I didn't think it would ever happen. There was the hope of not losing each other completely, but which one of us would make that call? Take that chance?

"The red apple," he said, crazily disarming once again.

"Big," I said.

In the end, it wasn't hard to leave. To pack up my bags along with all the hope and doubt I'd brought with me.

Twenty-four

Back in New York, the rush of the city was almost as foreign as the desert had been. But it was still the same, filled to the brim with people, the streets more crowded than ever, sparkling crisp and cold without bitterness. Life here had gone on, as it did everywhere, without me.

Exhausted, I knew I wouldn't sleep and called Thomas who showed up in no time with a bottle of welcome back champagne. We drank it all, all too quickly, and what with flying and funeral fatigue, fucking followed like a reflex. We made love like good friends, never ravenous, never oh-my-God. Instead of pulling at each other's clothes, we pulled back the fresh sheets on my bed.

"I've missed you," he said, afterwards.

Thomas noticed. He alone had missed me. "I appreciate that," I said. And, I did.

I closed my eyes, listening to the traffic ten floors below. I knew the city would slowly come back to me and in twenty-four hours it would be as if I'd never left. I had been ready to leave Australia and the outback, but I wasn't really ready to let it go. It felt too fast. Air travel between such disparate places never allowed enough time to decompress and properly transition.

Thomas was the good guy who waited. "You're dependable." I ran my hand along his thigh, more like a friendly pat than passion.

"Makes me sound like a Labrador retriever," he said.

It did. I hit his arm.

He barked. I laughed. So maybe this was it. I'd go back to work, find renewed joy, true fulfillment. Maybe. I moved my head on the pillow for another angle of the cracks on the ceiling, a map of Argentina, the Sicilian coast? Wherever I was, I always imagined being somewhere else, longing to be where I wasn't.

I pinned the sheets at my sides with both arms.

"So," he said. "Did you learn any great life lessons from traipsing to the other side of the world?"

"Sure. People die, nothing lasts. Big surprise," I said.

I hugged the sheets tighter. The apartment, empty for so long, still had that cool, unlived-in staleness. I didn't feel quite at home in my own bed.

Thomas reached across me for the single cigarette resting on the nightstand. "You gave it your best shot," he said. "I told you not to get your hopes up."

"I remember."

But maybe with time and proper editing, Cameron would have become the person, the father, or something close to it, that he'd never really been. Wasn't that the way it had worked for my mother? In her mind, he had been whatever she'd wanted.

I needed more, but of what I wasn't sure. Maybe I should leave the city for real. Go off somewhere and devote myself to a good cause. Of course, I could find that right here. And I'd tried it before. Helping. The trouble was I'd go straight from the local soup kitchen to worrying over which shade of lipstick to buy at Bergdorf's. So, now maybe it was time to get out of myself and do something worthwhile.

Thomas had put the unlit cigarette in his mouth. An ex-smoker, he enjoyed tempting himself. I pulled it out and crawled on top of him. Maybe I could tempt him, too. He was a big man and it was a haul.

"I need that," he said, looking at the gone cigarette.

I put my forearms on his chest. "You need this more." Wanting it to be better, I snuggled into his polar bear body, remembering Grant's hard angles and the smell of dirt and vodka and heated skin after sundown.

Thomas didn't put his arms around me, although I was working it, trying. The wine had worn off and playful lovemaking with a money manager wasn't easy. It was a mean thought. And unfair. There were probably women all over this city right now happily screwing bankers and economists.

I rolled away from him. "Sorry," I said, for both of us.

He turned his back to me, a move so unusual it sent a thin, cold ripple down my spine. Had there ever been a time when he hadn't responded to even my half-hearted advances? Something was different. I lifted myself on one arm and looked at him. He'd found the cigarette and was sucking on it again, his arms folded behind his head. His eyes were open, and I could see the wheels turning, his cool, calculating mind that made him so good at his job. I pulled the blanket closer to me when he suddenly threw it off, sat up, and started pulling on his pants.

"What are you doing?" I asked.

He was buttoning his shirt, slipping on his loafers. Goddamn fast dresser, I thought.

"This isn't such a good idea anymore," he said.

The chill I'd felt turned icy, my jaw tightened. Outside the window, a starless sky, a hidden moon.

"Let's stop kidding ourselves," he said, buckling his belt. "Or maybe it's you who should stop kidding yourself. I think I know who the hell I am."

True enough. I put a pillow over my head. "A three-piece suit," I mumbled.

"Speak up," he said, his voice raised.

I took the pillow away. "Like making love to a three-piece suit sometimes," I said, louder, wanting to hurt, throw the first blow.

"I'm going to allow for the fact you're jet lagged," he said. "But this suit's walking."

I sat up in bed. "Come on, I'm sorry."

"Don't be," he said. "Change is good."

"For what?" I asked.

He didn't say anything. Filling his pockets with keys, money, he finished dressing. I felt the colour drain from my face. Had I got it all wrong, had it been farewell champagne? Had he planned this? He came over and kissed me on the forehead like he was checking for fever, the forehead kiss of death.

"You need some time," he said. "I'm going to go before we hate each other."

I thought time was the one thing I didn't have, remembering Cameron telling me there would be plenty of it. I peered at Thomas like he wasn't really Thomas anymore.

"You're not serious," I said. Although it seemed he was.

"You'll do fine," he said.

I leaned against the pillows, nausea gripping my stomach. "Fine at what?" I asked, searching above, my arms flailed outstretched in supplication. Sleeping alone, eating alone? What could I do that would be so fine, cure the sick, end poverty? Had I ever done anything remarkable anyway, alone or not? Would I ever?

I turned toward him, watched myself watching him as he moved to the door. "Why don't you come back to bed?" I said, pathetically.

He looked at me without smiling. "I'll give you a call."

Not a new sound to me, a door closing. It was real quiet. Even the steady flow of traffic seemed to have stopped. Nothing moved until I slowly rolled over to the side of the bed and stood on legs not my own. Weak, conscious of each step, I wandered into the kitchen and looked out the window. Clouds floated between the buildings, obscuring whoever was inside and making me invisible, too. You can come back now, Thomas. Good joke, you got me.

I turned on the light. Too bright, I turned it off. On again. Face it.

Piles of mail were neatly stacked on the counter, courtesy of my elderly neighbour who didn't have one friend or relative left in the world, and I wondered how that felt, imagining myself old and alone. I could probably do one or the other, but both would be tough.

Inertia set in and I stayed where I was in the kitchen, shivering in my long tee-shirt and bare feet, mindlessly leafing through mail order catalogues. Grown men in roly-poly warm-ups and white-toothed nymphs in lacy lemon-coloured bras, everyone smiling. For a moment, I couldn't remember ever feeling so lonely. And then I could.

I traced the faint scar on the inside of my arm, a remnant of one of my last encounters with Stephen. An accident, I'd wanted to think. He'd been drunk, again, as we'd tried to out-tango each other in a fight to the finish we didn't know we were having. And where are you now, Stevie boy? Grant? Thomas? People die and are gone forever, but I hated losing anyone still above ground.

I glanced at the red kitchen stool I'd meticulously painted one useless Sunday. An imperfect job, I never failed to notice the brush strokes reflected in the glare of the overhead light. I should sand it down and do it over. Make it better. There was time for that. I could always make it better.

Epilogue

Time flies. It was still cold with the threat of a final spring snow, and I tried shaking my ill humour like a dog shakes off the rain. I bought a red wool scarf in an effort to look jaunty, although I'd never appeared jaunty in my life. I told myself to snap out of it.

It was a Saturday, nearly dark when I left the Metropolitan Museum where I went sometimes for the quiet comfort or just because I liked climbing the long, flat steps. From my position above Fifth Avenue, the city shined through leafless trees and I looked across town thinking I could see the last light on the river. Below me, people hurried by, wrapping coats tighter, holding hats against the wind. I walked down slowly, delaying the moment when I would merge with the crowd.

Stephen stood directly in front of me at the bottom of the steps, looking up at the museum, his hands in the pockets of his jacket, a tweed I didn't recognize. How strange that we no longer knew each other's clothes.

"Hello, Lils."

Unexpected and matter of fact. No one else had ever called me Lils.

So much time. And here he was. Look at us, breathing the same air. Hands still in his pockets, he leaned forward and kissed my cheek.

"I knew you were living in the city," he said, taking a step back, appraising me through horn-rimmed glasses.

He'd kept track of me.

"And you?" I asked, with a shaky voice. Could he hear my throat catch? See my apprehension?

He scraped his shoe on the cement like he was trying to remove gum. "I've been out of the country," he said.

And, out of your mind, I thought. He was still slim, although his face appeared fuller. Perhaps from alcohol, though he looked okay, not ravaged in the way it could happen. The edge of my coat flapped in the wind, reminding me of the tents in the desert. Maybe with more of a gust, I could fly up and get an aerial view: Lilly and Stephen, together again.

"I'm here to see friends," he added.

Who are your friends now, I wondered, friends like we had been? Best, forever?

Unable to form words, I shook my head in dumb nervousness, my hair blowing. Had he noticed how long it was? I brushed it back and glanced up the street. Did I look thinner to him, older?

He checked the time. "Could you have a drink?" he asked.

I hesitated, picturing myself drinking too much like we used to. I nodded and bit my lip.

We stayed on the park side of Fifth and walked to the St Regis, going against the wind. We had walked a lot of miles together and it occurred to me how natural it would be for him to slip his arm through mine, but he didn't, and we kept a steady pace and I a steady smile.

He talked about his work. He was painting all the time now and had some recent success with shows in Europe. I was glad for him.

We sat in big leather chairs in a corner of the bar, remodelled so it was the same but different. I ordered a martini.

"Nice coat," he said, as I slipped it off.

It was the closest thing to a personal remark he'd made. He hadn't asked me anything about myself, hadn't said I looked well, the way people do, being polite. He pulled out a small photograph and put it in front of me.

"My boys," he said.

For a second, I thought he said toys, and I stared at the photo of two young children as if they were something you wind up. They were nothing to me and he had been everything. His children had the same quizzical, arched brow look as their father.

"Sweet," I said. I handed the picture back to him and ordered another martini.

Stephen looked at his glass, and I looked at him. He was pale and the lines around his eyes didn't add character as much as fragility. He looked worn out. I wondered if he saw my own tiredness. Always missing someone could be exhausting.

"I went to China," he said.

"I was in Australia."

All those views not seen together. Had I missed the place for missing him? Had he? He would never know everything that had happened to me, this new history of mine. Just as I would know nothing of his. We'd both added to our individual narrative as our combined story faded to memory.

The room filled and grew louder. A striking woman in red sat motionless at the bar as the man with her worked his hand up her thigh and under her coat. She got dreamy-eyed and I looked back at Stephen who was twisting the ring on his middle finger, he'd never worn a wedding band. I suddenly wanted to make love with him. Crazy, but there it was. Women slept with ex-husbands all the time. I took the remaining olive from his glass without asking.

"I've always liked martini-soaked olives," I said, pulling it off the toothpick through my teeth.

"I remember," he said.

He remembered. I wanted to scream, you screwed up our lives. How could you? Instead, I slowly tried to get drunk, leaning across the table as he checked his watch for the tenth time.

"Do you have to be somewhere?" I asked.

"Dinner," he said. "Later."

"With your friends," I said.

He nodded.

I finished my drink. There were no hard edges now. I felt like I could glide right out of here and slither under the sheets. "Come home with me," I said.

The woman in red glanced at me, and I gave her a blank stare.

Stephen moved his glass in small circles on the table. "Why?" he asked.

"Because we'll probably never see each other again and we'll die unhappy," I said.

He touched my hand holding the glass stem.

"You're serious?"

"Yes," I said, serious and scared.

We didn't go to my apartment. We got a room upstairs, proximity was everything and we both loved hotels. The room was sumptuous, golden-peachy with subdued lighting lousy for reading and perfect for making naked bodies glow. We ordered champagne. Stephen uncorked it, something he was very good at.

I went into the bathroom, closed the door, and turned on the light of the makeup mirror, looking at myself encircled in soft fluorescent. The martinis had already taken their toll. I dabbed at my eyes, added lip gloss, and opened the door.

Stephen was on the bed propped by three pillows, holding a glass of champagne. He was fully-clothed, including shoes.

"California shit," he said. "Little better than rotgut." He was, after all, a connoisseur. "You get used to the French."

"Hmm," I said. Christ, I thought.

He poured me a glass and I sat, swinging my legs over the arm of a gilt and damask chair by the desk.

"Why don't you come over here?" he asked.

I took my champagne and climbed onto the other side of the bed. I had on wool pants, a sweater, and boots. Stephen put another pillow behind my back and we sat with our legs outstretched in front of us, listening to the wind whistle through the buildings. It was a sound particular to the city and when you heard it on the twenty-first floor, you knew how harsh it was at street level.

There weren't any right moves. We weren't like old lovers, familiar with every nuance. Too much time had gone by for that. And we weren't new lovers either, embarking on the future. We weren't lovers at all, were we?

Stephen put his hand over mine. So familiar, the thin fingers, the slight dark hairs, it was like looking at something I'd misplaced. He turned, touched my chin and lifted my head. Tears welled as melancholia set in. I blamed it on the wine, too sweet and sentimental. There was no way to hide. He put his hands on my shoulders, his touch intoxicating even through my heavy sweater. He looked at me, but I wouldn't meet his eyes.

"Couple of sad cases," he said.

"Comes and goes," I said.

"And never gone," he said.

"No, never gone."

I realised I was sober and didn't know why. Maybe our bodies take over when we threaten to lose our minds. I'd thought I wanted to get drunk and sleep with my ex-husband, but the desire I felt in the bar had turned cold as my body tried to save me from myself.

He reached up and turned off the lamp then reclined further on the pillows and I slid into him, resting my head against his arm.

He put his hand on my hair. "Long," he said, stringing it through his fingers.

We could make love, but I didn't think it would get any better. Why couldn't we just stay like this forever? To be found eventually, two corpses on a silken bed.

"I'm sorry," he said.

Uncommon words from him, but sorry for what?

For this moment, keeping our clothes on, unwilling or unable to be exposed once again? Or for what had happened before, growing apart, decaying so that all we had left between us was anger and then the other woman. What difference did it make? Sorry was sorry.

"I am," he said, touching my hand again.

"I know," I said. We both were.

We lingered, finishing the champagne, then put on our coats and rode silently down the elevator looking at our shoes. Stephen linked his arm through mine. The lobby glimmered in the reflected vanilla light of the crystal above. You should be happy in this place, I thought, wondering if I'd ever be back.

Outside, we stood on the steps above the flow of pedestrians and Stephen kissed me on both cheeks, so European for a guy from L.A. We put our arms around each other and held on, and I thought about how we'd never had a proper goodbye as though there were such a thing.

"I love you," I said, because it was true.

He said he loved me, too. His face close to mine, I felt the moisture on his cheek, his lips trembling imperceptibly. I started to walk away. He'll stop me, I thought. But, of course, I knew better. There was no stopping now. I kept going, moving faster, wanting only to turn around again and again. How could I do this? I'd held onto the possibility of seeing him for such a long time. What now? I pulled on my gloves, passing quickly through the crowd, lights blurring as I walked my no-nonsense walk into the night.

I headed uptown where couples, dressed for dinner

or the theatre, clung to each other, glittering, hopeful. Had they made love up in those honeyed hotel rooms? Through a burst of cold wind, I moved against the tide of just-released office workers. Women, hugging gym bags, rushed through doors swung open with happy-hour greetings as pinstriped businessmen, vying for position, disappeared amid whoops of laughter. The night was young, the world still spinning. I slowed down. There was always someone on the streets of this city in tears. A respectful glance and it was understood. Tonight was my turn.

Acknowledgements

First and always, to the late, irreplaceable, Les Plesko. With Les, I found a way to start, and without him, his wisdom guided me to the finish. How I wish he were here.

To my earliest readers, Stefanie Epstein, who called in tears late at night and gave me reason to hope, and to the late Malcom (Max) Stuart, agent, producer, neighborhood pal, who told me I was a writer. To close readers, Stephanie Kegan, Azarin Sadegh, and June Meyers, my deepest appreciation. To my precious writers' group: Patricia Albela-Silver, Laura Hubber, Patti Macdermott, Dana Mazur, Pegah Medhizadeh, Mary Presby, Azarin Sadegh. Serious, disciplined, and honest, you honour me with your insight and your friendship. To the wider group: Megan Francis Abrahams, Pamela Alster-Jahrmarkt, Jeff Darter, Ali Maclean, Jackie Lam. Always there in spirit. Thank you to Susan Henderson, magnificent writer, kindest heart, and the amazingly prolific, Caroline Leavitt, both unfailingly generous. To the wonderous Christian Kiefer, thank you doesn't say enough. And, to David Francis, Australia whisper, writer extraordinaire, your gracious friendship means the world to me, my gratitude is boundless.

Last, and best, to my family. To David, you're everything, always and forever. And, to Harvey, for sticking by me, giving me the treasure of time, and for your great understanding of a process that is often totally incomprehensible. I love you.

For an American writer to find a publisher in Australia where this book is set and where my heart travelled for so long, is simply perfect. Thank you, Jessica Bell and Vine Leaves Press. I started this book years ago and, like most books it went through many changes, as did I.

Vine Leaves Press

Enjoyed this book?
Go to *vineleavespress.com* to find more.